AHEAD OF THE CURSE

A CURSED WITCH MYSTERY: BOOK ONE

ELLE ADAMS

To be notified when Elle Adams's next book is released, sign up to her author newsletter.

1

"Perry, when I told you to bring the vampire into custody, I didn't mean in a body bag."

"You didn't say *not* to." I faced my supervisor across the cluttered surface of his desk, taking in the exasperated expression on his craggy green face. "It's the ideal way to carry an unconscious vampire around. Appropriate too."

"Not to the ordinary folks on the street who might have seen you disposing of a body," Kellen said sternly. "Undead or not."

"Nobody saw me, and isn't it better than the alternative?" At least a body bag was vaguely ambiguous. Unlike the vampire, who was currently snoring in the corner with his mouth wide open, exposing his fangs for the world to see. "I had to hit him with the knockout potion before he grabbed another human to snack on, and I didn't have a lot of options."

Annoyance furrowed his brow. "You know this is going to be a nightmare of paperwork for me, don't you?"

"Not if you don't mention the body bag part. It's not like they actually check up on these things."

Considering my boss was a literal ogre, you would think I'd be more intimidated by the exasperation lining his green face, but Kellen had known me since I'd been old enough to walk. He also knew as well as I did that when you were dealing with magical monsters, improvising was sometimes the best option at hand.

"And that isn't even getting into the two humans you knocked out in the process," he added.

"They didn't see me either. At most, they'll wake up with mild concussions."

Personally, I thought a concussion was preferable to being chewed on by a vampire, which would have been their fate if I hadn't flung the knockout potion directly at all three of them before our wily predator ran for the hills. There weren't many ways to subdue a vampire, let alone without tipping off the oblivious humans, which I thought my supervisor would understand. My job with the Wardens was to ensure humans remained happily unaware of their paranormal neighbours, which meant taking out transgressors and cleaning away the evidence before anyone was any the wiser.

Kellen sighed, and I sensed another rebuke on the horizon. "Putting that behind us for the moment, I actually called you here to give you some news on your next assignment."

I arched a brow when the vampire gave another loud snore. "More vampires?"

"No, it's a location switch," he answered. "You're being transferred to another office."

I blinked at him. "Already?"

I'd thought things had been going well recently, body bag incident aside. The Wardens had branches in all the UK's main cities and towns, and I'd bounced from one to another over the past ten years, but there were a lot fewer rogue vampires in my current corner of Manchester than there'd been when I'd arrived six months ago.

"That's right," Kellen said. "I've been in touch with a smaller branch of the Wardens up in Northumberland, and they're in need of a new member with your particular skill set."

"Northumberland?" I grasped at my admittedly patchy knowledge of geography. "You mean Newcastle?"

Newcastle was way up north, practically on the border with Scotland. Unless he'd meant to say Yorkshire instead, in which case I wouldn't have minded a stint in York or Leeds.

"No, I mean rural Northumberland."

"Rural," I repeated. "Yeah… no, that won't do. I'm a city girl through and through. You know that."

He did, too, since he'd been an intern for the Wardens in the very region of London in which I'd been abandoned by my birth family as an infant. Personally, I figured my aversion to nature was a side effect of my history because if I'd been dumped on a country lane, the odds of someone stumbling across me were not in my favour. As it was, my infant self had been found within minutes of screaming in an alleyway and taken into foster care. I hadn't met Kellen until a few years later, but he'd been handed the case file on my entire sorry history.

"Exactly," he said. "It'll be good experience for you."

"You and I have very different ideas as to what constitutes a good experience," I told him. "Rural paranormal communities can take care of themselves. They don't want outsiders wandering in."

"Ah, but that's where you're mistaken," he said. "Every paranormal community is unique, and I believe your skills are well-suited for this branch of the Wardens."

"What skills?" Staking vampires? Vamps favoured human prey, and there was a distinct lack of targets out in the countryside. Unless a vamp had taken to poaching a farmer's sheep, there was little demand for that particular skill. "I've worked at most branches already. What makes this one special?"

Aside from a lack of home comforts? My first foster placement had dragged me on a camping trip as a kid and it had been a disaster for everyone involved. Granted, I doubted my poor foster family had planned on us running into a nest of fire salamanders and the tent going up in flames, though they hadn't actually seen the little lizards. Instead, they'd assumed I was playing with matches.

Needless to say, I hadn't lasted long in that placement.

At the time, I'd assumed they were the anomaly and not me, but Kellen had set me straight on that one and informed me that most people did not run into weird magical critters on a regular basis. In any case, you'd think he'd have remembered that incident, given that it had led directly to our first meeting and my induction into the paranormal world, after which I'd sworn off exploring the Great Outdoors altogether.

Funnily enough, knowing the exact likelihood of running into a wild dragon or manticore didn't make the idea of camping in the wilderness any more appealing. Though monsters were the least of my worries as far as this new assignment was concerned.

"For one thing," Kellen answered, "you'll be living in a castle for the duration of your time working for the Northumberland branch of the Wardens. The castle was built in the Middle Ages, but it's fully equipped for modern living."

A *castle*? That one I hadn't seen coming. I'd visited a few castles over the years, but they tended to be crumbling ruins, not exactly habitable by modern humans. I wouldn't lie, the notion appealed to the part of me that liked the idea of dressing up in medieval armour to fight monsters. Some considered the Wardens the modern equivalent of mercenaries who dealt with paranormal threats in ye olden days, but Kellen's office was as dingy and mundane as you could get.

"Seriously?" I asked. "I'd get to live in a castle?"

My current rented flat was adequate compared to some of my past accommodations—which had included hostels with leaking roofs and bedbug-infested rooms—but it'd be nice to experience a little luxury for a change. Having a huge sprawling castle all to myself would certainly be worth the inconvenience of being surrounded by nothing but fields and farms for miles around.

"I thought that might change your mind." Kellen's craggy face split into a satisfied smile. "You'll start this weekend. What do you say?"

———

"This isn't what I had in mind."

I stood at the end of a gravel path, my broomstick in one hand and my wand in another, wishing I'd brought both an umbrella and significantly lower expectations. When Kellen had told me I'd been stationed to live inside a castle, I'd assumed he'd meant a massive medieval fortress. Not a small, squat tower formed of thick grey bricks with tall, narrow windows and a weather-beaten wooden door. It didn't look like the sort of place that had indoor plumbing or heating, let alone an internet connection or Netflix. Worse, it was absolutely bloody freezing in the northeast of England at this time of year, and drizzle hung in the air as if it wasn't the middle of summer.

But I forgot the weather when the sound of voices drifted through an open window, signalling that there were several people already *inside* the tower.

Perhaps the previous inhabitants were moving out on the same day I was due to show up, but the voices didn't sound as if they belonged to anyone in a hurry to leave. I didn't have a key, which seemed a massive oversight now that I thought about it, but I'd assumed the Wardens would have left it waiting for me inside the tower.

Grimacing when a droplet of rain fell down the back of my hoodie, I knocked on the door. Footsteps echoed inside, the thump of boots on hard stone, and I took an instinctive step backwards when the door swung inward, and I found myself nose to nose with the single most attractive man I'd ever laid eyes on.

Piercing green eyes studied me from beneath a furrowed pale brow, while his hair hung in silky curtains that were usually only seen in an ad for shampoo. Tall and lean—at five-nine, I rarely met anyone who could look down on me successfully, but he managed it—the man standing in the doorway might have walked out of a medieval novel himself. A medieval romance novel, that is, the sort with knights sweeping maidens off their feet and chivalry.

Of course, I was no maiden, and the guy didn't look like much a knight, either, once I got past his startling looks and took in his modern jeans and casual T-shirt. Did he not feel the cold?

He rested an elbow on the door frame and looked down at me. "Can I help you?"

I licked my dry lips. "I'm supposed to be moving into the tower today. I'm with the Wardens."

"You're the new team member?" he asked. "Peregrine Jacobs, right?"

"Just Perry, and—did you say *team member*?" At the sound of more footsteps on the steep stone stairs behind him, alarm began to rise inside me. "How many people are here?"

"Five including you."

My mouth hung open for a moment. Kellen had neglected to mention that I wouldn't get the whole tower to myself after all. Instead, I had to share it with an entire *team* of people, including a guy who'd rendered me speechless for possibly the first time in my life.

I closed my mouth and put my thoughts together. "Clearly, there's been a misunderstanding. I was told I'd be stationed in this tower for my next assignment."

"No, you're in the right place." He extended a hand. "I'm Tam. Team leader."

I looked blankly at his hand and belatedly realised he wanted me to shake it. As I did so, a spark zipped up my hand to my arm, the mild undercurrent of someone who'd either recently used magic or *was* magical. I wouldn't have taken him for a vampire at first glance, but the effect of his appearance on me couldn't be explained away by anything natural.

I released his hand and took a step backwards into the doorway. *I need to get out of here. Now.*

"Who's the newcomer?" Another man came into view down the staircase, tall and muscular with reddish-blond hair. This dude was definitely a werewolf.

"I'm Callum," he said in a Scottish accent, clasping my hand with a firm grip. "You're ... Perry?"

"That's me," I said. "I think I was misinformed on the, ah, nature of this assignment."

"What did your supervisor tell you?" asked Tam.

"That I was going to live in a castle near a town called —Hexworth, is it?"

"You're in the right place." The voice came from behind a door I hadn't seen behind Tam, which nudged open. A petite woman sidled out, her curly dark hair framing her pale face. A witch, I'd guess. "I'm Farley. Maurice is sleeping upstairs, but he'll show his face soon when he realises our new team member is here."

It was getting entirely too crowded in the narrow area at the foot of the stairs, but when I took a step back through the doorway, I found the drizzle outside had turned into a deluge. A sheet of rain poured down, instantly drenching me to the skin.

"You might want to get inside," Callum remarked. "Come on, we'll make room for you."

He retreated upstairs, as did Farley, giving me space to enter the narrow area at the foot of the stairs. Dripping and bereft of dignity, I closed the door behind me and promptly regretted it. The entryway was scarcely big enough for Tam and me to stand side by side, containing nothing but the wooden door Farley had come out of. The rest of the rooms must be upstairs.

"This way." Callum beckoned me to follow him and Farley up the steep stone staircase. Tam and I tried to go upstairs at the same time, resulting in an awkward collision of limbs that added yet another item to the list of reasons I wanted out of here as soon as possible.

As soon as the rain stopped, I'd be out the door faster than anyone could blink.

The stairs opened into a wide hallway that contained doors to the living room and a kitchen, while another staircase must have led up to the bedrooms. Plural. Given the tower's size, I ought to have known the Wardens were far too efficient to allow one person to occupy a single post. It'd been my mistake to assume otherwise, but I'd call Kellen and explain. He knew that misfortune was hardly unfamiliar to me and that there was a very good reason I moved between locations rather than settling down in one magical community. That way, nobody else had to deal with the fallout of…

Wait. Did my new team know about my past? I definitely needed to call my supervisor. Since the three of them were still looking at me, I put on a false smile. "I just need to make a quick call."

"Sure," said Tam. "We'll be waiting in the living room."

I made the mistake of looking through the open door and seeing the amber glow of a fire and several invitingly warm-looking blankets draped over the armchairs grouped around the fireplace. Sternly, I reminded myself of the reason they needed to light a log fire in the middle of summer and pulled out my phone. The quicker I sorted this out, the better.

Kellen answered right away. "I thought I might hear from you soon, Perry."

"Then you know what I'm calling about." I lowered my voice. "You know why I can't work with other people, much less *live* with them."

"I beg to differ." His voice took on the tone he used when he tried to convince me to take on unappealing cases, such as pixie infestations in public toilets. "You did fine in that shared house in Birmingham."

"If you forget the werewolf incident," I corrected. "And the tree that fell on our house."

"That was different."

"In what way?" I glanced up at the others, who'd settled into comfy-looking armchairs in front of the fire, and … was that a massive flat-screen TV? Irked, I wrenched my gaze away. "You know why it's unfair to them."

Nobody could agree on *what* kind of curse was on me, only that it was potent enough for me to require a warning label. Misfortune trailed me like a particularly loyal hound, often rebounding on the people around me, and if I admitted it to myself, part of me had wondered if being exiled to a castle alone had been an attempt to do the Wardens a favour. Which it might be, if not for the poor souls who had to *live* with me.

"I've been working with this particular team for long enough that I don't think that will be an issue," Kellen answered.

"Based on what evidence?" I hissed. "Besides, even if

we don't have any tragic mishaps, that doesn't mean we'll get along personality-wise."

"I expected that you'd say that," he said. "I think you need to keep an open mind, Perry."

"It's not my mind that's the problem." I'd tried to find a community that would accept me. Multiple times. Not only had I kept a hundred percent failure rate, but whenever the people around me learned about my curse, there was only one person to pin the blame on for all their misfortune. I didn't mind being a loner. Most of the time, anyway.

He drew in a breath. "This can be a trial run if you like. Stay here for a week or so, get to know the local community…"

"Is there one?"

"Yes, the village of Hexworth is a short walk from the tower."

"If they're anything like every other rural paranormal community I've visited, they won't be keen to make friends."

"Well, that's something you both have in common."

"Ha." Never mind the local community. At least I didn't have to share a *house* with any of the people of Hexworth. Sure, the three team members I'd met so far hadn't been unfriendly, but they didn't know me. Not yet.

When I glanced over at the living room again, Tam caught my eye for a brief moment. Could he hear us? If he was the sort of paranormal who had supernaturally enhanced hearing, possibly, but I'd already ruled him out as a vampire. Granted, if the last member of the team was asleep during the day, there was a fair possibility that *he* was one of the living dead, which would give me yet another reason to get the hell out of here. After the sheer number of vampires I'd had to haul into the office, living with one would be an exercise in extreme self-control I had no interest in participating in.

"Give it a try," he repeated. "I'll check back with you in a day or two."

"Wait a minute." But he'd ended the call, leaving me alone with three people who might have already heard me talking about how little I wanted to be here if my reaction to meeting them hadn't already clued them in.

Resigned, I shed my wet coat and entered the living room. The warm air wafting from the fireplace was as heavenly as it'd seemed from outside, but it didn't quite stifle the awkward silence.

"Hey," I said to the others. "Is there anywhere I can leave my coat to dry?"

"Sure," said Tam. "Leave it on the back of the chair."

I draped my coat over the back of an armchair, where it promptly dripped all over the wooden floor. "I need to get my luggage too."

Carrying a suitcase on a broomstick was an accident waiting to happen, so I'd left it in the hallway of my old apartment with the intention of using a conjuring spell when I arrived. Given the rain, I was glad I'd made that call.

When I reached into my pocket for my wand, and the others reacted as if I'd thrown a grenade into the room. Farley leapt to her feet, followed shortly by Callum, who moved protectively in front of her. Farley herself wore an expression that resembled a deer in headlights, as if she expected me to put a hex on her.

"Whoa." I lowered my wand. "I'm just fetching my suitcase. What's the deal?"

"Ah, we usually don't allow magic inside the tower." Callum met Tam's gaze for a second. "But I think we can make an exception, given how heavily it's raining out there."

"Of course." Tam hadn't got to his feet, but his manner had become notably more serious, even when Callum and Farley returned to their armchairs. "Go ahead, Perry."

What was that about? Did they have a bad experience with a rogue witch or wizard or something? I'd thought they dealt with monsters, not humans, but I hadn't exactly had the chance to ask Kellen for the details on my new team before I arrived.

Pushing aside my unease, I waved my wand and my suitcase landed at my feet. Simple enough. I pocketed my wand, but the others remained in a tense silence, and it was a relief to have an excuse to leave the room in order to take my suitcase upstairs.

"Yours is the room at the far end of the corridor," Tam called after me. "Feel free to take all the time you need to settle in."

The others had the distinct air of wanting to have a private discussion, and I was all too happy to leave them to it. But it didn't take a genius to figure out my new teammates might just be harbouring as many secrets as I was.

2

Once I'd hauled my suitcase to the upper floor, I took stock of my new room. It was cosy enough, despite the chill seeping through the stone bricks, and fitted with sturdy wooden furniture. At least I didn't have to share my bedroom with any of the others, so I'd have the huge wardrobe all to myself. Not that I needed to unpack since I'd be out of here within days, but it was a marked improvement on the moth-infested furniture of my old flat.

I left my suitcase at the foot of the bed and then had a quick snoop around the rest of the upper floor. The bathroom door stood open at the opposite end of the corridor, while all the other doors were closed. They must belong to the other team members, so I listened carefully to see if I could work out which room was occupied. I didn't hear a sound, but since vampires took the term 'sleeping like the dead' literally and didn't need to breathe, there might be one snoozing under my bed and I wouldn't have known any better. Never mind, then.

Moving carefully so as not to make too much noise, I tried each door one at a time. Two were locked from the inside, while a third had a key dangling from a padlock. A quick inspection told me it concealed a narrow stairway that led up into an attic and that the number of spiders present was far above my preferred number, which was zero.

Turning away with a shudder, I checked the last door, which opened, revealing the biggest room I'd seen in the tower so far. Easily twice the size of mine, the room had its own en suite bathroom and a huge four-poster bed dominating the wooden floor. A flat-screen TV stood against the opposite wall. Who got the upgraded suite? There wasn't anyone asleep in the massive four-poster bed, but a room of this size could only belong to the team leader. This must be Tam's room.

A creaking sound nearby made my heart jump in my chest. Hastily, I pushed the door closed and peered over the balcony to the floor below. Nobody had left the living room and nor had the fifth team member materialised, but a building this old was bound to be full of inexplicable noises. It wouldn't surprise me if it had a ghost or two as well, but I had enough trouble with the *living* inhabitants to worry about dead ones.

Steeling myself to face the rest of the team again, I went back downstairs. The murmur of voices from the living room hushed the instant I reached the door, and the whispers faded to silence. What were they being so secretive about? Unless they were talking about me behind my back, which was a fair possibility.

The sight of Tam brought a sudden rush of unexpected guilt for sneaking a look in his room. He'd left it unlocked, admittedly, but still. Clearly, I was already a pro at this team thing.

"Already unpacked?" he asked me.

Not exactly. "I'll deal with it later. Is there a mission on the schedule for next week? I assume there is since Kellen told me I'd be helping you out."

"Did he now?" His brow furrowed. "There isn't an official mission yet, but I sent in a request to take on a particular case, and I'm waiting to hear back."

"Doesn't your supervisor set the assignments?"

"Mostly, yes," he said. "This is a local issue, though, so I had to put in the application to the office myself. I assume you know all about the level of paperwork it takes to get a mission approved by the Wardens."

"Not really." Kellen sent me on missions, I cleaned up whatever needed cleaning up and he dealt with most of the paperwork. It worked just fine, without the need for a team hierarchy or whatever complicated setup they had here.

"Oh," he said. "Well, as a team leader, I get some leeway with which missions we get assigned to. I can submit my own suggestions, and I can also request that we prioritise a case that fits our expertise."

I hadn't known anyone other than supervisors got a say in what the rest of us did. Which meant, come to think of it, that I was technically without an assignment for the first time in my adult life. If it took longer to get the mission approved, what was I supposed to do with myself? The thought of being trapped in the tower for days with a bunch of strangers made my skin crawl.

"I'm sure it won't take that long to sort out," he added. "We're in a remote enough location that our supervisors sometimes have issues getting in touch. Storms can mess with the internet and phone signal."

Just what I needed. Given how far we were from civilisation, these people could be planning to murder me, and nobody at the office would be any the wiser. A paranoid thought, maybe, but with my track record, it wasn't *that* out there. Taking in a steadying breath, I told myself to get a grip. My supervisor knew my location, and it wasn't as if I was incapable of defending myself if necessary. Maybe not against four people at once, three of whose paranormal nature was unknown, but I'd faced worse odds.

It would help if I could figure out what Tam *was*. I squinted at him, then smoothed out my expression when I caught him studying my face. "You can't tell me anything about the mission before it gets approved? Wouldn't it save time later if I was already up to speed?"

Tam glanced at the others. Farley's shoulders had tensed, but Callum appeared unbothered. "I'm not sure on the rules since you're not an official team member yet," the werewolf said. "But you're a member of the Wardens, so I don't see why not."

Farley and Tam exchanged unreadable looks before the latter spoke. "I think we'll wait until we're all present before we start on the mission updates. As team leader, I'm supposed to help you settle in, as well as helping the others get to know you."

Get to know me? If they wanted my life story, then they'd be sorely disappointed. Especially as they seemed to be swimming in secrets of their own. "Can that wait until everyone's here?"

"Sure," said Tam. "Maurice usually shows up by early

evening unless we have to go out during the day. He's not much of a morning person."

Definitely a vampire, then. Hopefully, the others would have forgotten about asking personal questions when he did show up. In an effort to change the subject, I asked, "Does it always rain here?"

"It's relatively common, yes," said Tam. "If it wasn't so bleak out there, I'd take you for a tour of the area."

"We'll give you a tour of the tower instead," Callum offered. "You've seen most of it, I know, but not the basement yet."

"What's down there?"

"Our training room," said Tam. "Up here are the living room and kitchen, which are mostly self-explanatory. All the entertainment is in here. We have books, games, TV…"

"Netflix?"

"Actually, yes."

Another perk. Some of my previous accommodations hadn't even had crappy Wi-Fi, let alone the rest of this. Not that I was seriously considering staying put, however invitingly warm the fire might be.

"The kitchen … Maurice made a bit of a mess in there, so we'll show you that later," Callum said. "Upstairs are our rooms, the bathroom … oh, and the attic, but I wouldn't advise you to go up there without a light."

"What's up there?" I asked. "Not much except dust and spiders, I'm guessing."

"You don't like spiders?" Tam guessed.

"I don't mind them if they stay on the outside of the house. Or tower, as it were."

Callum grinned. "Same here. I'll show you the training room."

I followed him out of the living room and down to the lowest floor. The staircase was steep enough that walking around in the dark would be a health and safety risk, but at least it was a good workout. At the bottom, Callum pushed open the door Farley had stepped through earlier and revealed a cavernous room containing several treadmills, punching bags, and other equipment. On the opposite side were shelves and racks of various weapons, while a desk and chair occupied one corner. Above the desk, a corkboard had been affixed to the wall, on which someone had pinned an image of a map.

When I took a step closer, Callum moved in front of me, barring my view of the map in a manner that he likely thought was subtler than it was. "We should head back up to the warmth."

"Right." I was shivering, admittedly, but I made a mental note to come back for a proper look around later. I'd freely admit it was hypocritical of me to pry into the rest of the team's secrets when I had no desire to share any of my own, but my presence here was entirely Kellen's fault. Besides, trust went both ways. If they didn't share anything with me but expected me to do the same with them, then this wasn't going to work out for any of us.

I followed Callum back up to the living room, where Farley was flipping through the TV channels. Tam looked in our direction, his gaze questioning. "What do you think?"

"It's a nice tower." I wasn't lying either. In fact, it'd be close to perfect, if not for its other inhabitants. "More modern than I expected."

"It's belonged to the Wardens for decades, so they need to keep it up to date." Tam sounded pleased that I liked it. "It's within walking distance of Hexworth, but it's remote enough for a team to operate without constantly being stumbled upon by regular humans."

"Speaking of operations," I said, "do you normally stay local?"

"No. This is an unusual case." He pressed his lips together when Farley stopped channel-surfing to shoot him a wide-eyed look as if they were having a silent conversation that I wasn't privy to. They couldn't possibly think I didn't notice, surely.

"This meaning the current mission." The only way I knew to get to the point was to charge headfirst into it, and I might as well go all-out on my first day so there weren't any unwelcome surprises later down the line. "What's the big secret? I won't tell."

Mostly because I didn't have anyone *to* tell, except Kellen, and he'd already had the cheek to hang up on me. When nobody replied, I clarified, "I'm asking because I'm here to help with the mission. It's my job, after all."

In fact, I wouldn't say no to taking on a solo mission if it made things easier for everyone. If I asked permission, Kellen would hardly have a reason to object.

"Our mission is to investigate the death of someone from Hexworth," said Callum. "He was killed in the woods yesterday morning—" He cut off as Farley got up and left the room.

I frowned after her. "Something I said?"

"Obviously." The voice was unfamiliar, carrying a

strong Yorkshire accent, and I spun around to look for its owner.

The speaker was leaning against the wall as if he'd appeared out of thin air—which about summed up a vampire's silent approach. Tall and thin with a mop of dark brown hair, he wore a rumpled jacket and jeans that looked as if he'd slept in them. If I had to guess, he must have woken up when I'd been nosing around upstairs.

"Hey, Maurice," Callum said. "You're up early. Are you going to tidy the kitchen, then?"

Maurice scowled. "I was just on my way to do that."

"Sure you were." The werewolf's tone was light, teasing, which caught me off guard. A vampire and a werewolf living under the same roof was a rarity, much less actually getting along with one another. The vampire did wear a surly expression, but it appeared to be directed at me, not the werewolf.

I met his stare with a challenge. "Were you listening in on our conversation?"

"I didn't need to."

He *had* heard me creeping around upstairs, then. Vampires might be able to move with extreme stealth, but the faintest noise reached their sensitive ears. "What's that supposed to mean?"

"The kitchen," Callum repeated. "Go on, get it over with."

Maurice vanished, fast enough that I almost missed the blurred sight of him darting out of the door. Vampires were always such show-offs. Not to be deterred, I followed him.

Like the living room, the kitchen was a blend of ancient and modern. The worn table and benches might have been plucked straight out of the medieval period, while the microwave and dishwasher looked brand new. It'd have all been very snazzy and impressive if it wasn't for the three dead rats on the table.

"Ah." Callum had entered the kitchen behind me. "Sorry … that's Maurice's mess. He's kind of a slob."

"Thanks for that," said Maurice.

"Does he usually leave dead rats lying around?"

Callum grimaced. "Is that going to be an issue?"

I shrugged. "I've always fancied having a pet cat, and they bring in dead rodents all the time. This isn't that different."

The vampire shot me a glare, while Callum stifled a laugh. Behind them both, I could have sworn Tam almost smirked before he put on his usual professional exterior. "Clean it up, Maurice. Other people live here, and we have a newcomer to consider as well."

Maurice seemed even less enthused at my presence than I was about my own change in circumstances, which was saying a lot. While he sullenly began to clean up the dead rats, I addressed the team. "I'd appreciate it if someone explained how I spoke out of turn by asking about the current mission. That's why I'm here, isn't it?"

Maurice made a sceptical noise, holding a dead rat in each hand. "That isn't why. If I had to guess, someone wanted to get rid of you."

"Excuse me?"

That was uncalled for. Not to mention untrue. Kellen might put up with a great deal of crap from me, but I was one of his best Wardens—not to mention he was more of a father figure than a supervisor. The vampire was trying to push my buttons, though why he'd made such an objection to my presence was anyone's guess.

"Maurice," said Tam, in stern tones. "No need for that. We're still officially registered as a five-person team, and it was only a matter of time before the Wardens sent someone else in."

"What happened to your last member, then?" I asked. "Did they quit because of certain team members' bad attitudes?"

There was an awkward pause.

"She didn't quit," Maurice said. "Don't get too comfortable. You're here to fill a placement, nothing more."

"Were you this charming to your last teammate?"

"Maurice," Tam said, his tone even sterner than before. "Enough. You're being unnecessarily hostile."

"Only because *she* is," said Maurice. "Her thoughts are radiating hostility towards all of us."

Oh, crap. He could read my *thoughts*. How had I let his sudden appearance fool me into forgetting the other major advantage vampires generally had over the rest of us? Drawing on my training, I pictured blank stretches of stone wall in my mind, but I had the sinking suspicion that it was entirely too late. How much had he seen in my head?

Tam stepped in. "You know perfectly well that not using magic in the tower includes reading other team members' thoughts, Maurice."

"I didn't know she was a team member when I saw her," he said. "It doesn't matter. She won't be here for long."

"Not at this rate, I won't." I'd had about enough.

"Unfortunately, my supervisor has decided to wait a few days before letting me leave, so you're stuck with me until then. Sorry to ruin your day."

"What?" Callum's face fell. "Are you serious?"

Why did he look so hurt? "Since your teammate has already read my private thoughts, then I figured I might as well get it all out in the open."

"Oh." Callum's expression shuttered. "I didn't mean … I thought you were staying for the long-term. Maurice isn't all that bad once you get to know him."

"I've gone off the idea entirely." Once I started digging a hole, my mouth always decided I might as well keep going and continued to speak with zero input from my brain. "I'm willing to be polite and civilised towards him if he returns the favour. For the record, I don't have anything against the rest of you, but I'd appreciate it if one of you would give me a straight answer to my questions."

"Your predecessor died." Tam's tone was cool compared to his previous warmth, and for some reason, that made me feel worse than witnessing Callum's disappointment.

After a moment, his words sank in. "Died?"

Was that the reason for all the secrecy? I didn't need the details to guess there was a link with the team's reaction when I'd pulled out my wand, but for once, I had no desire to poke any further. Except where the mission was concerned. It sounded as if the team had been without a fifth team member for a while, but perhaps the case had stirred up bad memories, and my arrival had not helped matters in the slightest.

It would have been really nice if you'd given me some warning, Kellen.

"Yes," said Tam. "She died in the course of doing her job for the Wardens. As to your earlier question on our upcoming mission, I can give you the details if it makes you feel more comfortable. Like Callum said, a resident of Hexworth was killed while walking in the woods. His death was strange enough that we suspect magical involvement, but we're waiting for the office to give us the go-ahead to get involved with the investigation."

"Killed by a paranormal?" I guessed.

"We're not sure what kind," Callum said. "Not a shifter or a vampire, I'll say that much."

I glanced at Maurice, who'd disposed of the rats. Hopefully, he'd put them in the bin and not with the regular human food. While the Wardens would frown on him ambushing locals for sustenance, most law-abiding vamps paid discreet visits to local blood banks rather than snagging fresh meat. You'd think he'd have been worried about catching a disease, though vamps were immune to most parasites. The rest of us, however, were not.

Catching me watching him, Maurice scowled. "What?"

"Nothing." I turned back to the others. "If I understand this right, we need to find the culprit behind this murder and arrest them."

Tam arched a brow. "It usually isn't that simple."

No kidding. If a former team member had died on the job, the rest of the team would know the dangers first-hand.

In fact, it was no wonder Kellen had sent me here. He knew I couldn't bring any more misfortune upon their heads than what they'd faced already.

3

___

With answers in hand—to one question of the many on my list, at least—I returned to the living room with the others to make a game plan. Pity it was raining heavily enough to require a canoe to leave the tower because the forest where the man had been killed turned out to lie on the other side of the gravel path in front of the tower door. Practically on the doorstep. I could even see the outlines of the shaggy pine trees from the living room window.

Its proximity to the tower might explain why the mission was such a touchy subject with the others. Farley had yet to return from wherever she'd run off to, but Tam was all business now as he handed me a notebook in which he'd jotted down the basic details of the case. For a moment I debated taking it back to my room so I wouldn't have to look at Maurice's judgmental stare across the living room, but if he was trying to intimidate me into leaving, he'd be disappointed. I settled into an armchair and pointedly put my feet up on a footrest, flipping through the notebook while the others flipped through the TV channels and argued over what to watch.

According to Tam's neat handwriting, the victim of the attack had been hiking in the woods near Hexworth in the early hours of Saturday morning when he'd met a brutal end.

"He was stabbed," I read. "With a sharp instrument. You think there was magic involved, though?"

"I believe so," said Tam. "The police claimed there were traces of some kind of magic at the scene, but we have yet to look around the area ourselves."

"Traces of magic? You mean a spell, or—curse?" *Please not the latter.* I knew the textbook on curses backwards, but if I let too much information slip, a certain nosy vampire would know exactly how I'd come by that knowledge. "Was the victim a wizard? Might he have used magic himself?"

"Yes, but the police wouldn't know any better," Callum said. "Not that I can talk. I can sniff out a predator, no problem, but magic is another thing entirely."

"You'd be able to smell if a predator was in the forest, wouldn't you?" Shifters' senses were as sharp as vampires' if not more, especially their sense of smell. As far as I knew, Farley was the only other witch or wizard on the team. Tam didn't appear to carry a wand, anyway, though I was still in the dark as to his own paranormal status.

"I would," Callum said slowly. "But like Tam said, we don't have permission to go to the scene of the crime yet."

"Not even the outskirts of the forest?" If I were them, I'd have at least had a look around the part of the woods near the tower, but Tam struck me as the sort who always did everything by the book, and the others followed suit.

"Not yet, no," Tam said. "We ought to have a reply from the office by tomorrow morning, though. Then I can go to the police and let them know we're ready to help with the investigation."

His wording made it sound as if the rest of us would have to hang around in the tower until he got us permission to even *start* investigating. Not ideal in the slightest.

Maurice's attention remained on the TV, so I risked a question. "So—are there any suspects? People who might have been involved in the hiker's death?"

"The police have that information," Tam said. "Like I said, they haven't shared anything except the details in the notebook."

It was worth a shot. While I returned to my reading, Farley returned to the living room and sat down in an unoccupied chair. Her gaze briefly flickered to the notebook in my hands, but she didn't offer a comment.

As I read on, I found a more in-depth description of the victim's unfortunate death. According to the report, he'd been stabbed in the chest, and his heart had been cut out. The gory details didn't particularly bother me, but the police had found no traces of anyone else at the scene nor the missing vital organ.

Are they sure it wasn't a wild beast? The question lurked on my tongue, but the precision of the stabbing sounded far too exact for the average magical predator.

Monsters were one thing. The sort of monsters who wore human faces and lived among us were another matter entirely. Callum had already said it wasn't a were-wolf's work, but vampires didn't leave footprints, not if they moved swiftly and stealthily enough to avoid detection. Why would one tear out a person's heart, though?

They didn't need to rip open a person to drain their blood. No, I had to admit my spat with Maurice might be clouding my judgement … and on that note, I should probably avoid thinking too much on the subject while sitting in the same room as someone who could read my thoughts.

How had Kellen possibly thought putting me on the same team as a vampire was a good idea? My brain-to-mouth filter was faulty enough without the addition of a team member able to bypass that filter altogether and see right into my inmost thoughts. I gave it two days before one of us tried to throttle the other.

Giving the vampire another searching look—with no obvious signs that he'd heard my thoughts—I handed the notebook back to Tam. "So, what's the procedure? Wait until the rain stops and then go out to look at the crime scene tomorrow if the police give us permission to get involved?"

"If that's what we agree on," he replied. "The whole team gets a say, though the leader makes the final call."

Typical. "What are our other options?"

Other than staying in the tower and twiddling our thumbs, not much. Through the window across the room, the sky had already begun to darken. No surprise given the absence of any artificial lights save for the ones inside the tower itself, but the forest was reduced to a dark blur that might hide any invisible foes.

Granted, it was natural that I'd think the woods were creepy after I'd read the notes on the murder. Otherwise, I might have said the thick trees looked like a great way to trip over a tree root and break an ankle. Given the density of the forest, it might take a while to find the site of the attack, especially if the police had removed the body of the man who'd been killed. I did see a fancy-looking red car parked near the gravel path, but a few questions directed at the others confirmed it belonged to Maurice. It was a mystery why someone who could walk at the speed of light would need to own a car, but typical of the way my luck was going lately. Let's face it: I wasn't getting out of this tower anytime soon.

I turned away from the window when Tam lifted the TV remote and hit a button. The screen went blank, and Farley and Maurice both groaned.

"Now we're all here, I thought we could play a game." Tam nodded to me. "To get to know our newest team member."

No thanks. I really hoped he'd ditched the *get to know one another better* idea, but apparently not.

Maurice did not look thrilled either. "I was watching that," he objected.

"You'll have plenty of time to watch TV later when the rest of us are asleep."

Vampires and their odd sleeping schedules. "I'm good with watching TV instead," I ventured.

One would think Maurice would have been glad that I'd agreed with him, but instead, he glided to his feet with the grace only a vampire could accomplish.

"Where are you going?" Tam asked.

"Hunting."

"Didn't you already catch enough rats?" I asked before I could think better of it. "Hoping to add a spider or two to the collection?"

He grunted and made for the door, only for Tam to block his way. I blinked a couple of times, certain that he'd been nowhere near Maurice a second beforehand. How had he moved so fast?

Maurice's jaw tightened. "I thought we were free to do as we liked. It's our day off."

"Don't be difficult," said Tam. "I know for a fact you aren't going out hunting when it's raining like this. It won't kill you to be sociable for once."

"Nothing can kill the undead," Maurice said sardonically. "Fine, fine. Whatever you say, boss."

He zipped back to his seat and sent a disgruntled look in my direction while Tam reached for a worn pack of playing cards.

"We played a version of this game when we first moved into the tower," Tam said. "We each draw a card and the person who picks the highest number gets to ask a question of the whole group. I know only Perry's new here, but I think the rest of us could use a refresher on how to get along."

That sounded more like an excuse for my 'team' to prod me with unnecessary questions. In other words, as appealing as shovelling manticore dung. "Like a drinking game without the fun part."

Farley gave a slight cough. "I can get out the wine."

"No." Tam placed the deck of cards on the low table in front of the TV. "You remember why I set the rule against drinking games, don't you?"

"It's not fair if one of us can't get drunk," Maurice said in bored tones. "Got it."

Ah. Vampires were pretty much immune to alcohol, and I didn't need to give him any more chances to slip past my guard anyway. With reluctance, I drew a card from the deck when my turn came around. Farley went next, her expression unreadable, while I tried to puzzle her out. Callum was an open book, easy to read. Maurice's hostility was straightforward enough too. Tam… well, I didn't know what kind of paranormal he was, but I'd got a better handle on his personality than I had Farley's.

Not surprising, given that I was better at reading Ancient Greek than I was at reading people, and I'd never even spent more than an hour in a classroom in my life. Team games were not my thing at all, but if I had to endure this, then I might as well take the opportunity to learn some of the others' secrets.

Callum drew last, revealing the king of clubs. "I think I win."

"You do," Tam confirmed. "Which question do you want to ask?"

His brow furrowed. "Erm … my question is, where are you all from? You can say where you were born or where you've spent the most time. Up to you."

Even that was a tough one. I shrugged. "I was born in London, but I've lived in Birmingham, Manchester, a brief stint in Bristol, Cardiff…" I broke off when the others looked visibly surprised that I'd mentioned so many places, with the exception of Maurice. He'd already known. *Of all the people to poke their nose into my private thoughts.*

Callum answered first. "I was born in Glasgow, moved to Edinburgh, and then here."

"I was born in Cumbria," said Tam.

"I spent most of my life in Gloucester," Farley said easily.

When everyone turned to Maurice, he gave a

theatrical sigh. "I was born in York. Reborn there too. Happy?"

"Next round." Tam drew again, and the rest of us resignedly followed.

"Hey, I won." I held up the ace of hearts. "My question … what was your first job?" That seemed innocent enough.

Again, Callum was the first to answer. "I used to volunteer at an animal shelter."

"I waited tables," Farley said. "I also worked in a call centre for a bit. Frankly, I prefer dealing with monsters and murderers."

I couldn't say I disagreed. "I've never had any job except this one."

"Really?" Callum asked, surprised.

"Yeah, I signed up the day I turned sixteen."

I decided not to mention I'd worked with the Wardens for much longer than that. It wasn't strictly legal for them to let underage kids sign up, let alone access their monster-hunting gear, and my supervisor had made it clear that I wasn't to tell a soul that he'd bent the rules for me. Since school, magical or otherwise, had disagreed with me, there weren't many other ways to keep a highly-strung teenager occupied.

"Same here," Tam said to my surprise. "I signed up as soon as I was legally allowed to. Then I became a team leader two years ago."

"This isn't your first team?" I asked curiously.

"No, it's my first team, but we had a few members switch in and out." With a glance at Farley, he returned to the cards. "Next question…"

The game went on. When it came to basic questions, it

wasn't hard to give the stock answers I'd rehearsed over the years whenever I had to make polite conversation. Talking about books and movies were easy enough, but inevitably the questions took a sharp turn into unwelcome territory.

"Do you have any siblings?" asked Callum.

Oh, joy.

"Can we not?" said Maurice. "If I have to list every vampire my sire has ever created, we'll be here all night."

"He meant blood relations, you know that," said Farley. "I have a sister. Half-sister, technically. My mum remarried. We don't talk."

"I have three brothers," said Tam. "We're not close either."

Three? Just *one* of him was enough of a visual onslaught. You'd think spending an hour in his company would have lessened the impact of his startling, good looks, but my libido said otherwise. It was a good job *he* wasn't the mind-reader on the team ... though he *was* looking right at me. Wait, I was supposed to answer the question.

I dropped my gaze, giving a nonchalant shrug. "No siblings. There's only me."

"Really?" Callum's gaze filled with sympathy. "Hey, you can borrow one of my siblings if you like. I have six. Big shifter family. I have at least a dozen cousins too. I stopped counting at thirteen, to be honest."

I felt a rush of gratitude towards him for taking the attention off me, which I pushed aside. If not for this ridiculous game, he wouldn't have needed to come to my rescue.

"Maurice?" Tam asked.

Maurice begrudgingly said he had a brother—not of the vampire variety—and that he was no longer in contact with any of his other relatives. Not that unusual for a vampire, but I somehow didn't think it was his fangs that put them off associating with him. I was already starting to develop a headache from the strain of keeping him out of my thoughts. The instant I dropped my focus, he'd be able to slip in. I might have fought off a lot of vampires, but I'd never lived in the same house as one. Or castle, as it were. Far from giving me an insight into the others, the ridiculous game had given me zero ammunition to use against Maurice in the future.

With the cards put away, Tam asked a much more welcome question. "What takeout do you want me to order?"

"Chinese," answered Farley.

"We had that last weekend," Callum said. "Time for a change. Pizza?"

Maurice groaned. "The last one you ordered tasted like an old sock."

"More appetising than a dead rat, surely." Vampires could eat regular food; they just didn't get any actual nourishment from it and wouldn't die if they went without.

Callum looked amused at my comment, as did Farley, though Maurice shot me another dirty look. They soon delved into bickering about pizza takeaways, which was far more my speed than answering probing questions about my history. When Tam begrudgingly put the TV back on, I almost started to feel vaguely comfortable. The warm fire and blankets didn't hurt either.

"We should make a plan for tomorrow, right?" I asked

of the others. "Assuming we get approved for the mission, what time do we usually start? First thing, or when everyone's awake?"

I was trying to be considerate of the vampire's sleeping schedule, but he seemed to take it as an insult instead. "*You* can make a plan. I intend to spend the night watching TV."

Okay... "I thought the case was a priority."

I glanced over at Tam, whose attention was on Farley as if concerned she might leave the room again. Her shoulders had tensed, but she otherwise hadn't reacted to my comment.

"I'll call the police and check as soon as I've heard back from the office," said Tam. "We can't draw any conclusions of our own without visiting the crime scene."

"I guess not," Callum said. "It's worth making a plan, though. Like Perry said, we can ask the police for a list of suspects first. There can't be many people in the village who'd be twisted enough to cut out someone's heart."

Farley flinched, but she remained seated, gripping her blanket in both hands.

"You're sure the perpetrator was human?" I found my gaze straying to Maurice, my thoughts returning to my last mission despite my efforts to reel them in. A high percentage of mysterious deaths turned out to be victims of a vampire on the hunt, as my track record clearly showed. Granted, if Maurice lived on rats, he'd have no need to kill a random human in the woods. The notes hadn't mentioned the victim's blood being drained either.

Across from me, Maurice's eyes narrowed, and I glared back at him. If he didn't like what he found in my head, then it was his own fault for delving into my private thoughts in the first place. So much for settling in. If anything, though, I'd needed the reminder that certain other people were as resistant to my presence here as I was to being here at all. I didn't need to get too comfortable.

"We'll talk about it more tomorrow," said Tam. "Who's ordering the takeaway?"

"Me." Callum pulled out his phone and started asking for orders, while I connected mine to the tower's Wi-Fi in order to access the Wizarding Web. At least I had that simple luxury at my disposal, though I'd have given anything to return to my ratty old apartment instead. Moths flitted across the ceiling, while the dusty corners might have concealed any manner of eight-legged invader.

Spiders. I suppressed a shudder. Of course, an old tower like this would be a haven for arachnids, but my usual method of evacuating unwanted guests involved using my wand to catapult them outside. With the pesky no-magic rule, I'd need to think of an alternative.

Not that I was keen to give Maurice an opening to tease me about that irrational phobia by mentioning it aloud. The only spiders I could deal with were the giant monsters in the occasional online D&D game I took part in when I got a hiatus from dealing with real-life monsters. I played anonymously with strangers, which was more than fine with me.

I didn't need an actual team, complete with their own set of baggage. Yes, I'd promised Kellen I'd give it a shot, but he'd known the likely failure rate when he'd stationed me here. If I helped them solve this case, then nobody would have any complaints if I requested to be moved to a different location.

In the meantime, if the office dragged their heels on approving the mission, then they shouldn't have any objections if I took the investigation into my own hands. The storm would blow itself out overnight, with any luck, and I'd be able to go and have a proper look around the forest the following day.

4

That night, I passed out as soon as my head hit the pillow, lulled to sleep by the rain hammering in the background. The storm found its way into my dreams, however, in which I floated on a raft made of logs through a flooded forest. Shadowy trees loomed over me on every side, and while an ominous growling filled the background, I was never able to pinpoint the source.

Then when I turned around, I found I had company. Maurice stood silently on the raft, fangs bared—and when I reached out to push him into the water, I woke to grey light seeping through the curtains as dawn crept into my room.

Shaking my head at my own subconscious, I peered out the window. As I'd hoped, the rain had slowed to a drizzle overnight. Everything looked damp and unappealing, but I was pretty sure that was the default state up here near the Scottish border. I left my summer clothes at the very bottom of my suitcase and picked out jeans and a fleece instead.

After I'd showered and dressed, I went downstairs. Nobody else appeared to be awake at this hour, which wasn't a surprise since even vampires typically went back into their coffins by dawn. As nobody was in the kitchen, I had a poke around in the cupboards and swiftly concluded that there was cereal but no milk and that Maurice had indeed put the dead rats in the fridge alongside the dairy products.

Not exactly house-trained, is he? Shaking my head, I closed the fridge and contemplated the wisdom of going in search of a local shop to buy supplies from. The village must have one, surely. I pulled up a map of the area on my phone, finding that the fastest route to Hexworth involved taking a shortcut through the woods.

Hmm. Weren't the woods technically a crime scene? I hadn't heard from Kellen yet, but no doubt he'd be sticking religiously to his claim that I wasn't to call him until I'd taken a few days to settle in with my 'team.' I rose to my feet, restlessness stirring beneath my skin like an itch. If I opted to avoid the forest, the only other route to the village was the road, and I didn't have a car *or* a driving licence. I wasn't about to beg Maurice for a lift either.

Was walking down a country lane alone less dangerous than shortcutting through the woods? While the forest itself wasn't mapped in every detail, there were plenty of hiking trails. The whole place couldn't be off-limits, surely.

I grabbed my shoes and my waterproof coat and walked down the steep staircase to the front door. At the bottom of the stairs, I paused, hearing the repetitive thuds of someone thumping the punching bag from the training room. *Someone else is awake.* Odds were high that it was a certain vampire I didn't need another run-in with, so I left the training room alone.

I opened the front door as quietly as I could manage and stepped out onto the damp gravel path. The mass of trees at the end looked as inviting as a root canal.

This has 'horror movie scenario' written all over it, said a voice in the back of my mind. I might have paid more attention to the voice if pretty much my entire *life* didn't involve walking into situations that most people would describe as worthy of a horror movie. If I was the sort of easy victim with no survival experience, then ... well, I wouldn't be here to begin with, so it was a moot point. I had my wand, which was more than sufficient to handle any threat I might run into. I'd be fine.

I crossed the gravel path, a little surprised the others hadn't put more defences around the tower if there was really a killer wandering in the woods. Most people would think twice before attacking five paranormals at once, of course, but a lone hiker was an easy target.

On impulse, I checked my phone. My signal and internet connection had vanished the instant I'd left the tower behind. I'd have no way to reach anyone if I ran into trouble, but that was hardly a new experience for me.

I pocketed my phone and cast one last glance back at the tower, giving my misgivings a firm shove out of mind. I'd always worked alone, and the rest of my team clearly weren't in a hurry to start investigating the murder. There was no reason they couldn't have asked Kellen to accelerate giving them permission if the case was as urgent as they claimed. That on top of all the secrets they were keeping … no, I was better off going it alone.

Movement stirred in one of the castle windows, and I ducked into the woods, immediately surrounded by the shadowy pines. Raindrops showered me with every branch I brushed against, and I pushed a handful of damp brown hair from my eyes as I looked around to get my bearings. The nearest path went straight ahead. This must be the main track to the village, which was easy enough to follow despite the slippery mud underneath the leaves coating the ground where the rain had turned whole areas of the path into swamps. Gritting my teeth, I soldiered on.

Once the tower was out of sight, I started to wonder if I was playing it too safe. I'd intended to do some sleuthing, after all, and the attacker might not have stuck to the trails when they crept up on their target. Sure, the police hadn't given the team permission to investigate yet, but they would do so in a few short hours, and I highly doubted they'd be wandering around the woods at this hour of the morning.

Before I could think better of my decision, I pulled out my wand. A basic revealing spell ought to reveal any magical traces—maybe even a trail leading straight to the killer. No way to know until I tried.

I cast a quick revealing spell, but the swirling light from my wand dissipated without exposing anything. I walked a bit farther and tried again. Nothing. I needed to go deeper into the woods, closer to the site of the attack. Wherever *that* was.

The warning voice in the back of my head was more of a siren by this point, not at all helped by the dense trees and slippery mud I found when I left the hiking trail.

Plants snagged my legs, insects kept landing on my face, and leaves snagged in my hair. Nature had boundary issues, that was for sure, though I hadn't helped by wading into its midst. My next revealing spell cast a shimmering haze over the trees, which lingered in the air even after I lowered my wand.

Gotcha. Someone had used magic in the area, though it was too faint for me to trace. I trod forward into a clearing—and a burly man stood on the other side of the patch of trees, pointing a gun at me.

"Whoa." I stopped dead in my tracks, lowering my wand. "Who are you?"

"You're trespassing," he said. "You shouldn't be in here."

"You mean the forest?" Who was this guy? More to the point, what was with the gun? Most people in England did not keep guns for recreational purposes. Especially in the magical world, where a wand was more than sufficient for most witches and wizards. Had the traces of magic I'd detected come from him too?

"Yes, the forest," he growled. "You're not supposed to be here."

Well… he wasn't *wrong*, but that didn't mean I'd let him push me around. "Are you with the police?"

I had my doubts. He wore a baggy tracksuit, and his straggly grey hair looked as if it hadn't been combed in a decade. I might have pocketed my wand to show I meant no harm, but that would leave me unarmed.

"No, I live here. In the woods." His eyes narrowed. "You're not from Hexworth."

"I'm new here. I'm staying in the castle over on the other side of the woods."

He grunted, lowering his gun, but he didn't put it away. *Did he think he might need to shoot someone?* Paranormal hunters sometimes carried guns loaded with silver bullets specifically for dealing with rogue werewolves, but the hunters followed even stricter regimens than the Wardens did. There wouldn't be a lone hunter randomly living in the middle of the woods.

"I was just talking a walk," I added. "To the village."

"We don't want your sort in the village."

"Stanley." The voice came from the nearby bushes, and both of us spun in that direction. An instant later, Tam stepped into view, wearing a scowl I hadn't seen on his face before. "Calm down, Stanley. This is Perry. She's a new member of the team."

"Do you normally let your team members go wandering off alone?" Stanley growled. "I didn't know you gave her permission to come striding in here like she owned the place."

"He didn't." Once again, my mouth spoke before my brain could catch up. "What *is* your problem with me?"

"You need to ask?"

What was that supposed to mean? The woods were open to anyone, and he hadn't mentioned the murder, so his 'trespassing' comments were way off the mark. But if he had a touch of the Sight, then he might have picked up on the same vibe that sent most Seers running in the opposite direction when they looked closely at me. No, it was more likely that he'd taken offence at the very idea of a stranger walking near his home, but I didn't need another reason to feel as if the universe was determined to confine me to the tower.

"Regardless," Tam said, "Perry is part of my team, and

if you shoot her, I'm the one who'll have to handle the paperwork."

I *hoped* he was faking his lack of concern, but the sinking suspicion that I'd crossed a line in coming into the woods alone persisted when he didn't meet my gaze.

Stanley grunted in response. "Fine. I'll go, but only if you take *her* with you."

"That won't be an issue." Tam beckoned me to follow him. Getting the message, I turned my back on Stanley.

As we walked, Tam didn't say a word while I wondered why he'd failed to mention the guy *living* in the woods near where the murder had occurred. It was a major thing to leave out of his notes, if nothing else, but the team leader didn't speak until we'd returned to the path leading back to the castle.

"You shouldn't have come here alone," he told me. "What were you thinking?"

"I was thinking I wanted to buy something to eat that isn't dry cereal."

"We have a delivery scheduled for later this morning. Didn't I tell you last night?"

"Oh." Maybe he'd mentioned it the day before, and I hadn't remembered. "I forgot. Besides, I wanted to visit the town and check out the local area."

"You mean look at the crime scene." He didn't meet my eyes, but his voice was decidedly frosty. This time, I'd really ticked him off.

"I didn't intend to go out of bounds," I muttered. "I also didn't expect to run into a gun-wielding weirdo local who thinks the woods belong to him alone. What is he, a wizard?"

"Yes, he is," said Tam in clipped tones. "He's not the reason you shouldn't have been in the woods, though."

"I didn't think Maurice would appreciate me borrowing his car," I said. "It's part of my job to get to know the local area, isn't it?"

"It's *our* job, and I'm supposed to be responsible for your safety as long as you're staying in the tower. It'd be a black mark on my own record if you got yourself shot by the morning of your first day."

I blinked. "Wow, and there I thought it was my actual well-being that was your primary concern."

"I never said it wasn't."

My response dried up in my throat. What was I supposed to make of that? He'd certainly acted as if the worst part of Stanley shooting me was the extra paperwork, though that might have been a bluff. Who knew, maybe I was reading him all wrong, but this *team* situation was new territory for me in pretty much every way.

At least he hadn't asked what Stanley had meant by *your sort*, though I doubted it'd been a reference to the curse. The guy didn't strike me as all that perceptive, but my revealing spell had pointed to someone, and odds were, that someone was the forest's only inhabitant.

A murderer, though? I didn't know.

The rest of our walk back to the tower passed in awkward silence. I should probably apologise for my transgression, but the right words eluded me, and Tam didn't seem the sort of person who'd be satisfied with a simple 'sorry.' Let's face it, I was not a people person, and he confounded me more than the rest of my team put together.

Once we entered the tower, Tam made straight for the

training room, confirming that it was him I'd heard beating up that punching bag earlier. I might have gone in there myself if not for the distinct impression that he didn't want me around.

I didn't trust my mouth not to keep digging fresh holes to bury myself in, so I went up to the living room and browsed the Wizarding Web until Callum and Farley materialised, shortly before the promised supply delivery.

Tam reappeared to help carry in the various bags and boxes, resulting in a tense atmosphere in the kitchen despite the absence of their nocturnal companion, who must still be sleeping. I offered to help unpack the boxes and put their contents in the cupboards, and broke the silence by asking, "Who pays for the deliveries?"

"The Wardens do," Callum answered. "It's deducted from our salaries, but I reckon it's worth it. We usually have weekly deliveries, which is easier than sending people all the way to the village whenever we need anything."

"That and Maurice is the only one of you who has a car, and I guess you don't want him to be responsible for the shopping." I gave the nearest box a dubious look, wondering if it might contain vials of blood or worse. "There aren't any dead rats in there, are there?"

"No, Maurice does his own hunting," Tam answered, his silence as cool as it had been on our walk back from the forest. "I haven't heard from Kellen yet. I'll let you know when I do."

Callum gave me a puzzled look, while Farley frowned at Tam as she put two slices of bread into the toaster. I didn't have much appetite anymore, but I poured out cereal into a bowl anyway. Luckily, at that moment Tam's phone buzzed with an incoming call, and he left the room.

"What did you do?" Callum asked when the door closed behind him.

I poured milk on my cereal and didn't meet his gaze. "Went for a walk in the woods and got ambushed by its resident weirdo."

"Stanley? Oh, boy."

I put the carton of milk back in the fridge. "Our leader seems to have forgotten I'm not the mind-reader on the team. I couldn't have known there was a guy living in the forest if nobody told me."

"Sorry," he said. "I didn't think … I mean, I assumed you wouldn't go to the village without one of us."

"I wasn't blaming you. Just making a general comment." *Stop talking, Perry.* Why couldn't I stop making things more awkward than they needed to be? Callum seemed a genuinely nice guy, while Farley had been pleasant enough despite her obvious discomfort at my arrival here.

I carried my cereal bowl to the table and tried again. "I don't get why it bothered him so much. I wasn't anywhere near the crime scene, and I thought we could do as we liked when we weren't on missions. I would have gone out yesterday, too, if it hadn't been raining."

"I understand," said Callum. "You're new to the area. You wanted to explore."

"That, and I assumed everyone but our resident vampire was asleep," I added. "I didn't know Tam was a morning person."

Callum relaxed a little. "He's the boss. The only time he's not on duty is when we're all asleep."

"Guess I ruined his day already." I turned my attention to my cereal bowl. "I wouldn't have left the tower if I'd known it'd be that much of an issue."

"Nah, he's just overly concerned. You're the first new team member we've had since..." Callum lowered his voice when Tam came back into the room.

Since the last member had died. Oh. I'd forgotten, and in that context, Tam's reaction made perfect sense. When he looked at me, I wanted to shrivel up on the spot.

"Good news," he said. "Kellen called, and our mission paperwork is approved. We can go and talk to the police as soon as everyone's ready."

"We're going to Hexworth, then?" Part of me wondered if I was going to be confined to the castle in disgrace instead.

"We are. I'll just give the police a quick call first to let them know," he replied. "Everyone okay with that?"

"Of course," said Callum.

Farley didn't look too enthused, but she nodded. "Sure."

Tam's gaze lingered on me for an instant, making me feel inexplicably as if he was assessing my response. "Yeah, I'm in."

5

———

After breakfast, everyone assembled on the gravel path outside the tower. Tam was the last to leave, and after he locked up, he informed us that we'd be taking the scenic route along the road rather than the shortcut through the woods.

"Best give Stanley time to cool off," said Tam. "I don't blame him for being a little paranoid, given the circumstances, but we don't need to tick him off any further."

"You'd think the police would object to him pointing his gun at people," I remarked. "Unless he only does that to outsiders."

"He wasn't happy with us when we first moved in," Callum said to me. "Didn't point his gun at any of us, but I guess nobody had recently been murdered at the time."

Tam led the way off the gravel track and onto the road that eventually wound up in Hexworth. There was no pavement, but the lack of traffic meant it was safe enough to walk on the road. I had to admit it was an improvement on the forest, in which I'd constantly had to dodge insects and low-hanging branches, but Tam's frosty attitude cast a pallor over our group.

I fell into step with Callum. "How long has Stanley been living in the woods, then?"

"Longer than we've been in the tower," he replied. "He's pretty much a fixture there."

"Do the rest of the townspeople in Hexworth know he's living off-grid?" I asked. "And that he's liable to point a gun at any innocent hiker who happens to stray too close to his house?"

"No, he hasn't done that until … well, until you." An apologetic note entered his voice.

"That's nice," I said lightly. "There haven't been any other monster-related incidents in the woods before this weekend?"

"No," said Tam, overhearing. "We usually get sent to deal with cases farther afield, not this close to the tower."

He'd said as much the day before too, though if two days had passed since the hiker's death, one would think the police would have made a little progress on the investigation. One would also think a certain trigger-happy local weirdo watching for strangers in the woods would have noticed the disturbance too … unless he'd been involved in the murder himself.

That was my own paranoia talking, of course. If he'd been living there for years and hadn't attacked anyone before, then it seemed less likely that he was guilty of anything other than carrying a gun around—which I assumed he must have a licence for, but our encounter earlier might have ended badly for both of us if Tam hadn't intervened.

Maybe that was why he was still being so cold with

me. If I wanted to make any progress at all, I had to fix things between us. Somehow.

"Everyone in town is paranormal, right?" I asked of the others. "There's no need for us to hide what we are?"

"Everyone knows, yes," said Tam. "It's certainly easier to do our jobs when we don't have to hide our identities from the public."

"Yeah, I know the struggle." While there were pockets of paranormal communities in every main city in the UK, that didn't mean most people were aware of the world that existed alongside the ordinary one. Often, the hardest part of my job wasn't catching paranormal criminals or slaying rogue monsters but doing so in such a way that didn't violate the rules and expose our world for regular people to see. I'd hastily had to use spells on unwitting members of the public countless times—either to erase their memories of glimpses of the unseen or distract their attention so that they didn't witness me staking a vampire or knocking out a rogue shifter right in front of them.

"I bet," Callum said. "I usually have to refrain from shifting into my wolf form, which is a pain when we need to catch someone quickly."

"Yeah, that's why you went AWOL on that case when that rogue slipped the town's boundaries and ran into the countryside," Farley commented. "You ran in completely the wrong direction for miles."

Callum's expression turned sheepish. "In my defence, it was dark outside, and I can't always figure out directions when I'm in wolf form."

"Did you ever catch the rogue?" I asked curiously.

"Tam did," Farley answered. "Callum eventually got

back after we already had the guy secured and ready for arrest."

"Not my finest hour," said Callum.

I felt a twinge of curiosity about how Tam had single-handedly brought down a rogue shifter. Was it too intrusive to ask what kind of magical abilities he had? Normally the answer would be 'yes,' but he was the team leader, and the person I was supposed to trust with my safety.

Or stopping weird locals from shooting at me. On reflection, I decided to save that one for later. He didn't appear to carry a wand, at any rate, though Farley didn't either despite clearly being a witch like me. Wands were our primary weapon, but maybe she had some other gift that rendered it unnecessary. Tam, too, if he was a wizard at all.

The others began reminiscing about old cases they'd worked on, but I didn't mind not joining in that conversation. It was an improvement on the awkward silence, if nothing else, and without Maurice doing his best to antagonise me, the atmosphere was more amiable. The area was picturesque, too, with fields of grass and heather dotted with patches of forest and ramshackle farmhouses.

We reached Hexworth without any more run-ins with the locals, and Tam led our group down a cobbled street into the village itself. The collection of stone buildings was small even by paranormal community standards, consisting of one post office, one convenience store, one bank, and a few other essentials for a paranormal community like an apothecary and a shop that sold wands and other accessories.

The police station was smaller than our tower and

contained a grand total of three staff, led by a grey-haired, stern-looking woman who carried a steel-coloured wand in her belt. Two equally surly wizards staffed the desk.

"And who's this?" The woman looked down her nose at me when I walked in with the others.

"This is Perry, the newest member of our team," said Tam. "She's here to help with the investigation."

"I see." The woman clucked her tongue, while one of her associates gave me a dirty look from behind the desk. That was friendly. What was their problem? They couldn't possibly know about my spat with Stanley in the forest already.

"Perry, this is Janessa, head of the local police," Tam said. "I think it's better if the rest of you wait outside."

I abandoned any hope I might have had of the villagers being any friendlier than old Stanley had been and followed the others out into the cobbled street, leaving Tam to talk to Janessa alone.

"Don't worry about her," said Callum in a low voice. "She took a while to warm up to the rest of us too."

"I suppose it's an improvement on having a gun pointed in my face." I lowered my voice when one of the officers gave me another glare through the glass door. "Does everyone here distrust outsiders?"

"Pretty much," he said. "Like I said, they'll get over it if you stay long enough."

He said the last part without meeting my eyes, bringing a twinge of guilt at the reminder of my outburst yesterday. I'd said I intended to get out of here as soon as possible, which remained true, but I wished I'd put it more delicately. Not that I'd had many options after Maurice had gone riffling around in my thoughts

… and if the morning so far was an indication of how my week was going to go, they were better off without me.

The awkward silence persisted until Tam opened the narrow door and exited the police station. "Good news. Everyone is up to speed, and we have full permission to be involved in investigating the hiker's death."

"Does that mean we're going back to the scene of the crime?" I wasn't enthused about the idea of entering the forest with Stanley still sniffing around, but I'd need to go back if I wanted to follow the trail of magic to its source. If the team leader agreed, of course.

"Not yet," Tam said firmly. "Janessa has also given us permission to talk to any potential suspects, and there's someone they want to invite in to be questioned later today. She said I can pass on the message. This man has been in trouble with the police in the past, apparently, and he was friends with the victim."

"Then he's a suspect?"

"No, there's nothing to directly link him to the case," said Tam. "But when you break the law in a small town like this, the police take notice. We can ask him a few questions while we're letting him know Janessa wants to speak to him. What do you think?"

"Worth a shot," Callum replied, and Farley nodded in agreement.

I'd be defensive, to say the least, if a group of strangers came into my house and started asking questions, but it was better than fielding glares from the local police offi-cers. "Sure."

Tam led the way down the cobbled street with Callum and me behind him and Farley bringing up the rear.

"Are you sure he'll want to talk to all of us at once?" Callum asked, voicing my own question aloud.

"That, I don't know," said Tam. "Ordinarily, we'd all split up and go to talk to different possible suspects, but his is the only name Janessa gave me, and the link to the case is tenuous, to say the least."

"Some of us could look at the crime scene instead," I said casually. "To avoid overcrowding him."

Tam looked askance at me. "I already told you we aren't going into the forest."

I raised my hands. "Hey, I didn't mean me specifically. Besides, what are we going to do if this guy turns out to be a dead end?"

"I'll decide." Tam walked on, while I wished I hadn't spoken at all—and for that matter, that I hadn't gone into the forest earlier and ticked off Stanley at all. If I hadn't, then Tam might have agreed with my idea rather than shooting me down.

Callum gave me a sympathetic look while Farley let him overtake her. "For the record, I'd be twitchy if four strangers came to interrogate me."

"That's what I thought." I fell into step with her, more to avoid catching Tam's eye than anything else, though I had to wonder why she'd voluntarily come to help with the questioning when the case clearly bothered her. Or so I'd assumed given her reaction the previous day when I'd brought up the subject, though it helped that we no longer had Maurice hanging around making barbed comments.

"Have you met many of the locals?" I asked her.

She shrugged. "Nope. Tam told you we've never had to investigate anything in Hexworth, didn't he?"

"Yeah, but I figured you needed to come here for supplies."

"We order most of our stuff online," she said. "Hexworth is too small to find anything but the most basic essentials."

"And they don't like outsiders," I added. "Including this guy we're meant to be questioning, I'm guessing. Why did he end up in trouble with the police in the past?"

"He was selling illegal potions online," Tam answered without turning around. "He got away lightly with a warning because they couldn't find proof that he'd brewed up anything too dangerous."

"But the police kept his name on record?" This was a prime example of why living in a small community was my idea of hell. Everyone was constantly entangled in one another's business, and keeping secrets was an impossibility. Unless you lived in the forest and pointed a gun into the face of anyone who got too close, that is. I assumed everyone made sure to give Stanley a wide berth.

After we rounded a corner, Tam came to a halt outside a crooked stone house in dire need of roof repairs. He knocked on the red-painted door a couple of times before a dishevelled wizard with curly red hair answered, wearing what appeared to be a dressing gown.

"You're Reynard?" asked Tam.

"That's me," he answered. "You selling something?"

"No, we're with the Wardens."

"What's that?"

He didn't know who the Wardens were? Farley hadn't been kidding when she'd said most of the locals weren't familiar with us or our work, but I'd have thought he'd have recognised the name at the very least.

"We're here on behalf of the police," Tam clarified. "Officer Janessa asked me to let you know she wants to talk to you, but I'll let you get ready first."

"Why's she sent you, then?" Reynard backed into the hallway. "Can't be bothered to call me herself, can she?"

"She asked me to come here because we work for the Wardens," said Tam with more patience than I would have demonstrated if I'd been in his place. "We're consultants on a particular case the police are investigating. Namely, the death of a local man you're known to have been friends with."

His eyes rounded, the truth of his dilemma sinking in. "You better come in, then."

The narrow doorway opened into a living room that smelled strongly of the sort of herbal concoctions one might expect of someone who dabbled in illegal potion-making in his free time. A box filled with dubious-looking bottles containing brightly coloured solutions confirmed he hadn't kicked the habit that'd almost got him arrested once before, but there was a world of difference between selling dodgy potions and committing cold-blooded homicide.

Reynard vanished upstairs and left us crammed in the box-sized living room, and I wished he'd asked us to wait outside instead. The scent of herbs made my eyes and nose itch, while Farley broke into an uncontrollable coughing fit.

"Got a remedy for that in the box on the right," Reynard called downstairs. "The red potion'll sort that cough right out."

"No thanks," Farley wheezed. "I'll take my chances."

"Suit yourself." The sound of doors slamming echoed above our heads. "What's Janessa want with me, then?"

"You knew the victim of the murder on Saturday morning?"

The slamming noises ceased. "Sure, I knew him. Good man."

"The police want to question you because you've been in trouble with the law enforcement in the past," Tam went on. "For brewing illegal potions and selling them online. Is that true?"

There came a thud and a curse from upstairs. "Well, that's nonsense, isn't it?"

"You know the laws, I assume."

"Nonsense, like I said," he grumbled. "Nobody should be able to control what I do in my own house. You tell Janessa that."

"Tell her yourself," Tam said. "We're not here to talk about the potions, besides. What were you doing in the early hours of Saturday morning?"

"Saturday?" he echoed. "I was on a hiking trip."

Tam raised a brow. "At four in the morning?"

"A *camping* trip," he corrected. "I like to go out walking in the hills. The fresh air clears my head, know what I mean?"

Given the suffocating smell of potion ingredients inside his house, I'd wager he'd need to get outside to be able to breathe at all.

A moment later, Reynard came thumping downstairs, dressed in a mangy-looking waistcoat. "Right. I'm ready to talk to that interfering old bat."

"Thanks for cooperating." Tam strode out of the room, and the rest of us gladly left the cramped house behind.

While Reynard locked his front door, Tam turned to the rest of us. "I expect Janessa will check up on his alibi."

"You want to go to the police station while she questions him?" I asked dubiously.

"No … I don't think that'll be necessary." Tam watched Reynard totter away down the street. "I doubt he'll have anything more to say to her, and if he gives himself away as the killer, then it'll be Janessa's job to take him into custody."

"*Do* you think he's the killer?" I asked curiously.

Farley broke into another coughing fit. "If he's still selling those potions, he might be a killer several times over."

"Cutting out someone's heart, though?" Callum shook his head. "I didn't get that vibe. Especially if he was friends with the victim."

Hmm. "Did the police have any other suggestions?"

Callum shook his head. "Doesn't sound like it, right, Tam?"

"No." His gaze travelled from Reynard's house to its neighbours. "I can't speak to the hiking alibi, but nobody else was found in the woods except for the victim."

And Stanley, I silently added. "Did the police comb the whole forest?"

"To the best of their ability, which isn't saying much." Tam's mouth turned down at the corners. "I had to give them a copy of our map to pinpoint the scene of the crime, and frankly, I think we know the forest better than they do."

"You mean we have to go there ourselves?" Farley asked. "To the scene of the attack, I mean?"

"I think it's our only option," Tam said. He didn't meet

my eyes, which made me wonder if he'd expected me to respond with an *I told you so*, but I said nothing. It didn't feel much like a victory to be so bereft of any clues whatsoever that we had to walk into the forest and risk running into Stanley … or worse, the monster itself.

Regardless, it was time for us to look at the scene of the crime.

6

The nearest entrance to the forest lay on the border of the village, separated from the houses by nothing but a low wall of crumbling stone that looked as if it'd been there for centuries. The four of us climbed over the wall and found ourselves surrounded by towering pines, with several visible trails extending deeper into the woods.

Tam surveyed the forest for a moment and then indicated one winding path. "That's our quickest route to the crime scene."

He'd memorised the map? That was impressive, though it might have been a necessity given the lack of any access to GPS out here. I could barely remember the way down the village's one main street, let alone the forest's winding trails.

"Are you certain?" Callum asked. "We don't want to end up walking in circles."

"The main hiking routes are well-marked," Tam said.

"Also, if anyone has anything they want to say before we go in, say it now. We don't want to draw attention."

"From Stanley," I surmised. "Whereabouts does he live? I mean, how deep in the woods is his house?"

"His home isn't too far from Hexworth, but we aren't heading in that direction," said Tam. "He tends to wander around the woods, though, which is probably why he was near the tower."

That didn't count as much of an excuse to me. He'd had no reason to be walking that deep among the trees, nor for his irrational response to running into another person when he knew full well the tower was inhabited. Of course, he hadn't known me for a team member at the time, and I'd also had my wand out. That probably hadn't helped.

I put the question of Stanley aside before I drew Tam's ire again. "Did the attack take place nearer to the village than to the tower?"

"I think so," Callum replied. "From what I remember of the spot we marked on the map, but we left it back in the training room."

So that was what he hadn't wanted me to see during our tour the previous day. "Didn't the police remove the body? How will we know we're going in the right direction?"

"I'll know," Tam said. "We'll need to search the surrounding area too, in any case. Not just the scene of the crime."

"It's okay for me to use magic out here in the woods?" I asked, just to clear up the matter. "I can cast a revealing spell to expose any magic that was used recently, but I understand if that's too flashy."

"Not at all," said Callum. "I can't sniff out magic, so we need an alternative."

"Don't look at me," said Farley. "Perry, you're the only one of us with a wand, so someone has to do it."

Huh. She'd confirmed that Farley and Tam didn't carry wands. I'd already suspected Tam was more than a regular wizard, but I would have thought Farley would want to protect herself from any threats.

I'd save the questions for later because the longer we stayed here chatting, the higher our chances of encountering Stanley again. "Good. I'll do that, then."

"Sure," Tam said. "We'll go straight to the scene. Everyone, try to keep quiet from now on."

My nerves spiked inexplicably as we made our way down the path leading into the heart of the woods. Most of my apprehension was centred on the possibility of running into Stanley again, which irritated me more than anything else. I didn't scare easily, but having a gun pointed in my face had been a new experience, and so was trekking through a creepy forest that might be hiding a killer. All my past cases had been in cities, or towns at the very least, and the absence of any background noise but our own footsteps brought a peculiar sense of isolation despite the presence of my teammates.

Farley must be nervous too, because she jumped at every small noise until she came to a sudden halt. "Do you hear that?"

"Hear what?" asked Callum. "Is someone else here?"

"I think so." She stood on tiptoe, rotating on the spot. Tam followed the movement with his gaze, as did Callum, while I kept my eyes wide open for Stanley and his gun.

The forest remained silent until a large man dressed in what appeared to be a suit of armour loomed out of the bushes. I reached for my wand, while Tam moved in front of the rest of us as if to shield us from the giant sword the man held in both hands.

At least until the handle fell off, and what was left of the sword fell into a sad, crumpled heap. The man blinked up at our group. "That's the trouble with cardboard. Not built for the weather."

The sword was made of cardboard. So was his armour, now I looked closer, its silver paint smeared as if he'd recently walked through a swathe of sopping wet leaves.

"What are you doing out here, Karl?" Tam asked in an exasperated voice.

He knew this guy? How many more resident weirdos could one tiny village possibly have? Granted, dressing in cardboard armour and wandering around the woods with a giant sword was a step up from pointing a gun in my face, but he'd better have an explanation at hand.

"Sorry, I was practising," said Karl. "Didn't mean to startle you all. Is the whole team here?"

"Almost the whole team." Farley gave him a disgruntled look. "You take this role-playing thing way too seriously, you know."

Ah. If he was part of a local LARP gathering, the rest of his group appeared to have gone walkabout, then.

"Why are you in the forest?" asked Callum. "Didn't you hear about the murder?"

"Murder?" Karl echoed. "No. Who got murdered? When?"

"A hiker was killed on Saturday morning," Tam

replied. "In the early hours. I thought everyone in the village knew by now."

"I was at a convention all weekend," said Karl. "I got back late last night. Why, did the murder happen somewhere in the woods?"

"Yes," Tam told him. "We're helping the police investigate the man's death, and I'd advise you to stay at home for the time being."

The colour drained from Karl's face. "I didn't know. Are the police looking for people to help search the forest? I know these woods inside and out."

"No, they aren't," Tam said. "We're helping out because the police think this is a matter that might need the Wardens' expertise, but they don't want civilians involved."

"Then I wish you the best of luck." Karl broke into a jog, armour and all, and vanished among the trees.

"Oops," said Farley. "Sorry for the false alarm."

How had she heard him before the rest of us had? Callum was the one with a werewolf's enhanced sense of smell, though the scent of damp leaves permeating the forest might have dampened his usually sharp senses.

"No worries," said Callum. "I didn't expect to find anyone in here—except Stanley, of course. How'd Karl manage to miss the news?"

"Looks like he misplaced the rest of his role-playing group too." I knew better than to judge people for their hobbies, but the news of a brutal murder must have spread like wildfire in a village as small as Hexworth. "Is it just me, or were all the suspects conveniently out of town when the murder happened?"

"I wouldn't call him a suspect," said Tam. "Karl might be a little absent-minded, but he's always been polite whenever we've spoken."

"Is it a novelty when someone doesn't hate outsiders by default, though?" I queried. "I don't know the guy, but it seems odd that he'd pick here to practise sword-fighting. He must be confident Stanley won't mistake him for a threat and shoot him."

"Shh," said Callum. "He might be listening. We're near his home after all."

We were near Stanley's house? Intrigued, I scanned the area, but I didn't see any signs of human habitation. "If he hasn't heard us, he must be wandering around elsewhere."

Near the tower, for instance.

"Yes, and we should keep our voices down." Tam stepped into the lead again. "Let's move."

I followed, keeping both eyes open for any signs of other interlopers. The notion of Stanley roaming near the tower wasn't appealing, but if he woke up Maurice and the two got into a standoff, it'd serve both of them right. Despite Tam's insistence to the contrary, the old wizard remained at the first spot on my suspect list, and I halted mid-step when my gaze picked out a large, hunched shape on the other side of a large swathe of trees that resembled a shed or cottage. *That's got to be his house.*

The man himself didn't appear to be around, so I took a step forward—then Tam's arm blocked my path.

"Don't," he said. "I know what you're thinking, but don't."

"I just wanted to have a closer look, if he isn't there…" I trailed off when he grabbed my elbow and brought me to a standstill. His grip was surprisingly strong. "Okay, okay, message received."

He let go of me, and we continued to walk, Callum and Farley both avoiding my eyes.

After a short pause, Tam spoke. "I know he isn't around, but his house has magical defences all around it. It wouldn't surprise me if he added even more after the murder. He's a little paranoid, if you didn't already notice."

"Noted." I could dismantle most security spells with my eyes closed, but not necessarily without alerting the person who'd set them up in the process. For all I knew, he was lurking in a bush nearby, ready to shoot anyone who stepped out of line.

"Also," Tam said, "if you did take out his defences, he'd know it was one of us. Nobody else in town has that skill set, and it's not worth the risk to the rest of the team."

"Fair enough." Thoroughly chastised, I didn't so much as glance behind me at the house as we walked away, though I did wonder how far Stanley would have to go before the others considered him a suspect. If Tam was as much of a stickler for the rules as my supervisor, as I suspected he was, he'd want everything done according to procedure with the police handling the actual arrest. I'd have no hope of convincing Janessa to haul Stanley in for questioning based on a simple hunch based on his behaviour towards me.

We walked in silence for several more minutes while I pondered on how Reynard's interview with the police was going. Dodgy potions aside, he still ranked below Stanley on my suspect list, but if they were a starting point, I'd barely scratched the surface of Hexworth's bizarre inhabitants.

Tam brought us to a halt and pointed to the right, whispering, "We're here. You can leave the path, but don't go too far into the woods."

I took a hesitant step forward, but this time he didn't stop me from entering the mass of trees bordering the path. Thick pines shrouded a clearing where a bed of leaves covered the muddy ground, not quite concealing the bloodstains spreading from a spot in the middle of the clearing.

This is the place.

Once I looked past the blood, I saw no discarded weapons nor any footprints, though the soil was churned up around the clearing, and the sprawling tree roots might have concealed anything. Soon, my boots were caked in mud, and the scents of rain and damp leaves were thick in the air. I spied Callum sniffing at the clearing's edges, but he shook his head when he caught me looking. "I can't smell a predator, and I can't identify any humans either."

I reached for my wand and then hesitated, glancing towards Tam. He gave a nod, offering permission, and I cast a revealing spell.

A cloud of smoky green light billowed into the air, and a tingling sensation travelled up my arms as if I'd pressed my fingers into an electric current. The light spilled across the ground like water from an overturned bucket, overlaying vibrant symbols arranged in a circular pattern. I recoiled, nearly dropping my wand.

The place was drenched in dark magic. The symbols

made my head swim with nausea, but I forced myself to focus on them, trying to see if I recognised any.

The light died out when my spell faded, taking the symbols along with it. Behind me, Farley sucked in a breath. She'd turned her back on the clearing, her hands fisted at her sides, while Tam and Callum both looked on in puzzlement.

"What's there?" Callum gave me a concerned look. "What's with those markings?"

"I think," I said, "the victim was sacrificed."

"What would make you say that?" Tam asked, his gaze searching the clearing before focusing on my face. "What did you see?"

"Symbols etched in a circle." I gestured up and down the clearing. "A summoning circle, which means dark magic. The murderer must have killed their victim and offered his heart to … well, to whatever was on the other side."

Tam muttered a curse under his breath. "I suppose the murderer didn't expect anyone knowledgeable on the subject to stumble across the scene."

"You'd think anyone who knew we lived in the tower would have guessed." Unless, like Stanley, they'd intended to prevent us from getting into the forest altogether. "Though I'm guessing the locals aren't that well-versed on the Wardens, considering that Karl had no idea anyone was murdered, and Reynard didn't even know the Wardens existed at all."

Someone had been responsible, though, and the question of *why* lurked at the forefront of my mind. Generally, a summoning involved an exchange, or an offering, to something from the place known to most as the afterworld. The killer had slaughtered a man to summon an unknown creature, meaning the beast must be on the loose in the woods. No wonder Stanley walked around carrying a gun.

Unless he was the person who'd performed the sacrifice to begin with. It would explain why the beast, whatever it was, had left him alone. My skin crawled at the thought. Farley looked as if she might faint, and Callum had gone pale as well.

"I think we should get out of here," he said.

"Agreed." Tam glanced up at the sky, which had darkened in the short time we'd been in the woods. "Looks like another storm's on the way. We need to tell Maurice what we found, then make a plan."

I didn't argue. There was nothing else to see, and the drizzle began in earnest as we continued down the path back to the tower.

When we reached the other side, the rain intensified without the shelter of the trees. It came as an unexpected relief to reach the tower and get in out of the cold dampness, though that relief vanished abruptly when we found Maurice was awake. He sat at the kitchen table with a wine glass in his hand, sipping a dark-red liquid that I suspected was not chardonnay, despite the bottle on the sideboard next to him.

I arched a brow. "You store your blood in wine bottles? Really?"

"That's right," said Maurice. "You all went to the village without me, did you?"

"I thought you wouldn't be awake until later," said Callum.

"Perry here's an early riser," added Farley. "Like Tam."

She'd relaxed a little upon entering the tower, though she'd hardly said a word since our trip to the forest and my gruesome discovery at the clearing. Taking a seat next to Maurice, she kicked off her muddy shoes.

"Sorry we left you out," Tam said to the vampire. "I got a call from the office this morning giving us permission to start our investigation, and I wanted to visit the police in person to ask more questions."

You aren't going to mention the sacrifice? Maybe he meant for me to break the news to the vampire myself, given that I'd exposed the dark magic at the scene, but Maurice's irritation at being left out wouldn't improve if he learned I was the one who'd picked up on a clue about the murder. Besides, I didn't need him to learn of my humiliating encounter with Stanley earlier.

"As for the rest," Callum put in, "we'll tell you when we're done with lunch. Assuming anyone's hungry."

I wasn't, and not just because of the unappetising sight of Maurice with blood all around his mouth and the even less appealing thought of what might be roaming in the woods, unchallenged.

While I removed my coat and boots and made coffee, I let the others bring Maurice up to speed on our chat with the police, our brief visit to Reynard, and our trip through the woods on the way back.

"So let me get this straight," he drawled. "You had our newbie cast a spell at the crime scene and believed her claims about the murder being linked to a ritual only she seems to know about. How do you know she wasn't having you on?"

I glared at him. I'd been focused on keeping the vampire from reading my thoughts, but if there was one thing I hated, it was being called a liar. *Have fun with this, then.*

I looked Maurice directly in the eyes and thought of the symbols on the forest floor, focusing on the way they'd spread across the clearing in oozing, malevolent lines. It brought a sweep of nausea, but Maurice's eyes widened a fraction.

Then Farley fell out of her seat in a dead faint.

Tam snapped into action at once. He lifted Farley off the floor and carried her upstairs to her room, while the rest of us looked on in bewilderment. Or I did, anyway. Callum's expression was more akin to concern, while Maurice was outright smirking.

I knew I'd screwed up somewhere, but I couldn't begin to figure out how showing him my thoughts had caused her to pass out and not him. Hadn't Farley already seen the markings for herself in person? She'd turned her back, admittedly, but her reaction hadn't been anywhere near as strong. Unless…

"Is Farley a mind-reader?" I asked Callum in a low voice. "Did she read Maurice's thoughts, and that's why she passed out?"

"No … she isn't," he said. "You'll have to ask her yourself. It's not really my place to share."

My face burned. "I really didn't expect that to happen."

"I know you didn't." Callum shot Maurice a warning look when the vampire made a sceptical noise. "Maurice, make yourself useful and clean up. You've spilled blood on the table again, look."

The vampire gave a shrug and wiped the blood off the table's surface with his sleeve. *Ugh.*

Annoyance sizzled below the surface. If he hadn't called me a liar, I wouldn't have felt compelled to show him my thoughts, so this entire situation was as much his fault as mine. If he didn't stop smirking, then he'd be the next person needing to be carried unconscious to bed, so I left the kitchen before I lost my cool and clocked him in the face.

Tam's voice drifted from above. Not wanting to bear witness to his disappointment yet again, I made for the stairs leading down to the training room instead of going up to my room. The large room was unoccupied, giving me ample opportunity to test out the treadmills and weight machines. Imagining the punching bag was decorated with Maurice's smirking face kept me entertained for a bit, but my gaze kept straying towards the desk in the corner.

The map pinned to the corkboard above the desk did indeed depict the forest, with a single pin marking the centre. If I had to guess, that must be the spot where the murder had taken place. *Or rather, the ritual.*

I moved closer, seeing that old Stanley's house wasn't marked on the map, but the village was sketched as a cluster of buildings south of the mass of trees. I was snooping again, but I'd all but estranged myself from the rest of the team already, so I might as well have a look around the team leader's desk. A laptop and plug sat on the desk below the corkboard, but the drawers underneath were padlocked shut. No surprise, but I had to wonder if records of past missions were locked in there. Had the team ever come face to face with a sacrificial ritual before? Questions bounced around my skull, mostly centred around their odd reactions to those symbols.

Had Maurice recognised them? Had Farley? Leaving the desk, I returned to the punching bag. Giving the others time to cool off—and Farley time to recover— seemed the only viable option, but if we didn't return to the case soon, the murderer might kill again. It was safe to say the police hadn't seen the markings since they were only visible with the aid of a spell.

I debated calling Kellen, but he'd made it quite clear that I was supposed to wait for longer than a day before checking in with him. If he was familiar with the rest of the team, did he know what Farley's problem was?

The thought brought another twinge of guilt, but it wasn't unreasonable to want to avoid accidentally triggering her again, was it? My own curiosity was only a small part of it, though as this whole fiasco had made abundantly clear, I was not a team player by any stretch of the imagination.

Regardless, calling Kellen felt too much like giving up.

The door moved inwards with a faint creak, and I released the punching bag, letting it swing to a halt.

"Thought you'd be in here," Tam said.

I didn't quite manage to meet his eyes. "I don't know what happened back there, but it wasn't intentional."

"I know," he said. "Farley does too. Don't worry."

I gave a half-hearted punch and caught the bag before it swung back and hit me. "If Maurice still doesn't believe me, I'd be more than happy to take him to the scene myself. I can't promise to bring him back in one piece, though."

"He was baiting you," said Tam, disapproval entering his voice. "I told him not to do it again. I also made it clear that disbelieving one another is not how we work here. If we can't trust each other, we haven't a hope of achieving our goals."

The intensity in his tone disarmed me. Sure, he was team leader, but he couldn't seriously think I'd ever dream of trusting *Maurice*, did he? Perhaps it explained why he and Callum had been so disappointed at my vehement desire not to fit in with the team, but I knew a lost cause when I saw one.

"I think that ship has sailed," I said. "Not only sailed, but it's sunk to the depths of the ocean and become infested with sea monsters."

"I think that's a slight exaggeration, Perry."

I drew in a breath. "Tam, I understand that you're the team leader and you need to give everyone a fair shot, but I've never been part of a team before, and to be honest, I always thought my supervisor wanted to avoid placing me with anyone else. You can probably guess why that is."

He gave me a considering look. "Try me."

Huh? What was that supposed to mean? "You want me to list out the reasons that I'd be better off moving into a hut in the woods like old Stanley than trying to fit in here?"

He didn't react to my reference to the grumpy forest-dwelling local, to my surprise. "I think it might help both of us know how to move forward if you tell me. I'm the team leader, remember, and I can't fix problems if I don't know what they are."

"I don't think I'm going to like this game."

Adding to my bewilderment, he chuckled. "It's not a game, but we can make it into one if you like."

I stared at him for a moment. It certainly felt like a game to me. I'd screwed up in a dozen ways in the course of a single day, but he still wanted to give me a chance. The rest of my team, though, would beg to differ, and I knew better than to think I'd get through this case without burning through all the goodwill I had left.

"Where to start?" I began. "I wasn't prepared for this, which is entirely my supervisor's fault and nobody else's, including yours. I came here expecting another solo mission. I'm not used to having to take four people's feelings into consideration… at least one of whom hates my guts and can also expose my inmost thoughts for the world to hear." I clamped my mouth shut, knowing I'd already said too much.

"I've told him not to do that," said Tam. "Maurice claims he didn't try reading your mind today until you showed him what we saw in the woods."

"That's hard to prove." I shook my head. "More to the point, he already soured the rest of the team's opinions on me by telling them I was considering getting out of here. If I changed my mind, then it'd be too late, wouldn't it?"

"And have you changed your mind?"

My mouth parted. "Even if I had, I'm pretty sure Farley wants me gone as much as Maurice does. That leaves you and Callum, and the latter is friends with Maurice, isn't he?"

"That doesn't matter." A hint of impatience entered his tone. "We could all do with making fewer assumptions about one another. I include myself in that. I assumed

Maurice would be more open to the idea of a new team member than he turned out to be, and while we didn't get much warning, that's no excuse."

"Kellen's fault, again," I said. "I really can't fathom why he decided to drop this on me. If he was trying to straighten me out, he's about ten years too late."

I'd been running solo since I was sixteen, for crying out loud. Maybe I'd been redeemable as a teenager, but not now.

"I don't think that's true," Tam said. "There's always an adjustment period when we have a new team member. Farley and Maurice were both the same when they first joined up, believe it or not. Only Callum settled in right away."

I could see that, but that didn't change the fact that they'd had years to get to know one another. "Did Maurice start out by reading *their* thoughts?"

"Forget Maurice," he said. "Aside from him, do you think you can learn to trust the rest of us?"

My mouth parted. At least *he* couldn't read my thoughts, though if he'd tried to do so at the present moment, he'd find nothing but a massive question mark. "Honestly? I have no idea."

"That's a start. Just keep an open mind."

"I'll try," I said delicately. "But there's still a lot I don't know about how things work around here ... and about the team."

Tam's lips compressed. "If you have any questions, then I'll do my best to answer them at any time. Unless they breach another team member's privacy. I find we work better with a certain level of trust between us, but as team leader, it's not my place to break confidence with the others."

Translation: he wasn't going to tell me Farley's secret. I'd have to ask her myself. "Okay."

"Good," Tam said. "Also, what I said about privacy applies to you too. If Maurice reads your thoughts again, then he knows I'm not going to let him off lightly next time."

From the warning note to his voice, I believed it. He might not have been forthcoming with the details of his own skills, but my instincts told me the guy was dangerous. He'd become a team leader for a reason, and I wouldn't deny that part of me was intrigued enough to almost regret that I had to leave.

When I was gone, though, it didn't matter what secrets he was hiding. I had no intention of staying. That hadn't changed, and yet part of me wondered all the same.

"That's all I wanted to say," he said. "Like I said, keep an open mind, ask questions if you have them, and try not to antagonise the rest of the team."

"I'll try." Easier said than done. Normally when I disliked someone, it was easy to avoid them. Not so much when we lived in the same building.

"The same rule applies to the others," he added. "Can we put everything behind us, and start over?"

"I guess."

He extended a hand. "Let's start again. I'm Tam."

"Perry." I shook his hand, bemused, and felt another odd electric tingle. Not the sort that came from a spell, or the darkness I'd sensed around those markings in the forest, but something else I couldn't put a name to.

"Short for Peregrine," he added. "Interesting choice of name."

"I picked it out myself." Wait, why had I told him that? "I thought you were going to say it's a guy's name."

"No ... except in the case of a certain hobbit."

"That *may* be where I got the idea." That he'd figured out the reference caused him to climb several levels in my estimation, though I failed to mention that my first foster family had originally called me 'Prudence'. Needless to say, I'd shed the name as soon as I'd been old enough to watch *The Lord of the Rings*.

"You have good taste in movies," I told him.

A genuine smile tugged at his mouth. "We'll have to watch them one night if I can get the others to agree."

He hadn't given a time frame, but at least we were allies now. For the purposes of solving the murder, maybe it was better for me to accept I wasn't going anywhere for the time being. "So ... what now?"

"I'll take you to see Farley."

"She's awake, then?"

"She is, and like I said—there are some things you're better off hearing from her instead of from me."

If she was willing to share, of course. The brief warmth that had blossomed from our moment of connection was already beginning to chill at the prospect of talking to the others again. I'd promised to try, though, so I said, "All right."

With reluctance, I left the training room and followed him upstairs. The sound of the TV drifted from the living room. Callum and Maurice must be in there, but neither of them came out when I walked past. Good, because I didn't need any witnesses to my fumbled attempt at an apology, especially ones with fangs and a bad attitude.

Tam led me to the upper floor and halted outside a partly open door to one of the other bedrooms, indicating for me to go ahead. I peered through at a room the same size and shape as mine, though a little more lived-in. Clothes hung on the outside of the wardrobe, and a stack of comic books littered the floor. I suppressed the impulse to withdraw when Farley sat up on the bed, looking directly at me.

She tilted her head at me. "Aren't you going to come in?"

I drew in a breath and pushed the door open farther. "Erm, I just wanted to apologise for … for whatever I did."

She rolled her eyes. "Tam made you come and talk to me."

"He didn't make me, he asked me nicely." I remained in the doorway, so she didn't see the team leader waiting outside to prove her point. "I think we got off on the wrong foot, but I won't do it again. Whatever I did."

She snorted. "Wow, he really freaked you out, didn't he?"

"No, you freaked me out, not him." Wait a moment. "Not you specifically, just the fainting thing. It worried me."

So much for not screwing this up.

Farley pulled a face. "There's nothing worse than facing awkward apologies. Maurice's was bad enough, but your discomfort is making me twitchy. Chill out."

"So, you *are* reading my thoughts?" It was rare, but not unheard of, for witches to have that ability. I'd never met one who did, but there was a first time for everything.

"I wish," she said. "No, I'm an empath. I pick up on the emotions of everyone around me. Good and bad."

"Really?" I hadn't expected her to give me a straightforward answer, much less one that made so much sense. "Everyone? At the same time?"

"Yes—and no," she said. "It depends on how strong the emotions are. Everyone has been on edge because of the murder anyway, and then you showed up…"

"At the worst possible time, I know."

"Not really," she said. "Murder investigations are always tricky. I can't be around anyone directly connected to the victims or else I get swamped in their grief. And when someone gets a sudden jolt of emotion, it can hit me like a truck. Handy sometimes, but mostly a nuisance."

"That's why you passed out?" I thought back. "Whose emotion hit you?"

"Maurice's."

"What, I actually shocked Maurice?" I asked. "All I did was show him an image of what we saw in the woods. He didn't seem that bothered on the outside."

Why had it shocked Maurice so much to see the images? If he'd been anyone else, I might have understood his reaction that someone had used magic to sacrifice another's life, but you'd think a vampire would have seen much worse.

"He's a vampire. They're good at hiding what they're feeling."

That wasn't news to me, but a flicker of suspicion stirred inside me despite my best efforts. Had he recognised the ritual in some way, or had his shocked reaction been directed at me for exposing the marks, which were supposed to remain unseen?

I shut down the thoughts before their accompanying emotions reached Farley. "I'll try to avoid doing it again in future. I didn't want him reading my thoughts anyway, but when he didn't believe me…"

"No, I get it," she said. "You wanted to show him the proof."

"Yeah… I guess it can't be easy living with someone as grumpy as he is."

"Nah, it's fine most of the time," she said. "I've had a lot of practice distinguishing others' emotions from mine, but it can be hard when someone new joins the team because I don't yet know their temperament or how they're going to play off the other people around me. That's why I left the room when you wanted to know the details of the murder."

"I guess it hasn't helped that Maurice and I have been arguing all the time."

"You should have seen him and Callum when they first moved in together. I thought we were going to have to assign them separate floors."

"They didn't get on?" I thought of the laid-back were-wolf. "Was Maurice still leaving dead rats everywhere, then?"

"Pretty much. With Callum being such a neat freak, they were bound to come to blows. It wasn't until Maurice saved Callum's life on a mission that he began to chill out a little."

I turned this over in my mind. "If I have to save his life to win his esteem, he might be waiting a long while."

She studied me with a slight frown. "I thought you were leaving. Did Tam talk you into staying?"

"I'm… considering the options. Starting over." Impulsively, I reached out a hand. "Let's start over. I'm Perry."

"I'm Farley, and I don't do handshakes."

"Oh." I dropped my hand. "Because touching another person gives you more access to their emotions?"

"See, you're learning already."

Tam peered into the room. "Ready to come downstairs?"

"Only if you have something to eat," said Farley. "I'm starved."

"Callum's making lunch, so yes," he said. "I've put Maurice on washing-up duty."

I laughed in surprise. "As long as he's washed the blood off his hands first."

"Could be worse," Farley said. "He used to put his bloody wine glasses in the dishwasher before we convinced him to wash them by hand."

"Lovely."

The three of us headed downstairs, me feeling more optimistic than I probably should have. Not only had I finally made some headway with the team, but with all of us on the same page, we might finally be able to make some progress on investigating the murder.

Hey, I could dream.

8

My optimism wasn't entirely unfounded. While the rain refused to abate, leaving us confined to the tower for the rest of the day, the team took the 'starting over' theme to heart—with the exception of Maurice, whose sullen silence was at least an improvement on our earlier fighting.

Farley had relaxed entirely now that we'd stopped sniping at one another, while Callum reacted to the revelation about the origins of my name by promising a LOTR-themed movie night later in the week. The others enthusiastically agreed—except Maurice, though I inferred from his interactions with Callum that he would have agreed with the idea if it'd been suggested by anyone but me.

All in all, it was a successful evening despite the storm raging outside, which persisted long into the night. As I tried to sleep, rain battered the windows, and the wind crept through gaps in the stone walls, echoing above my head as if there was a drunken bat colliding with the walls. I'd wrapped myself in as many blankets as I could pile onto my bed, but the chill still crept through, while the windows rattled in their frames as if someone were knocking to come in.

No doubt that was the reason that when I did eventually fall asleep, the draughty windows followed me into my dreams. A figure crouched on the windowsill, the rain blurring their features, but I recognised Maurice.

"Nice try, but I'm not inviting you in," I said, raising my voice over the howling wind. "You can stay out in the rain."

Maurice bared his teeth, pressed against the glass. Then his figure morphed into Stanley, his gun pressing against the glass. He pulled the trigger—and a loud crack jolted me awake.

I sat upright in a tangle of blankets, my heart racing in my chest. *What was that?* It wasn't a gunshot, but it was *loud* and came from the direction of the forest. More cracking noises followed, quieter than the first, followed by a low, animalistic growl.

My instincts kicked in. I leapt out of bed and grabbed my wand from the bedside table. My window overlooked the back of the tower, not the forest, so I slid my feet into my shoes and grabbed my jacket for warmth before leaving my room.

The pitch-blackness of the upper floor greeted me, a trickle of moonlight streaming through the dusty window at the far end. On swift feet, I crossed the upper floor, holding my breath at every creak of the wooden boards underfoot until I reached the window overlooking the forest. The trees were reduced to a blur of darkness, so I cast a quick spell to create a small ball of light. I'd broken the *no magic inside the tower* rule, but the last thing I wanted to do was panic everyone, especially as I now knew that we had a mind-reader and an empath on the team. The growling noise might have belonged to a regular animal, but my instincts said otherwise.

By the light at the end of my wand, I could make out the shapes of trees amid the darkness—and the reflection of a silent figure standing behind me.

I spun around with a hiss of alarm, my improvised ball of light illuminating a wide-eyed Tam. He pressed a finger to his lips, not offering a comment on the hovering light, his gaze fixed on the window.

Heart hammering, I looked outside again. The trees appeared a little lopsided. The first cracking sound might have been the wind knocking a tree down, but the growling was more difficult to explain. Despite my hovering light, I saw no signs of threats—monstrous or otherwise.

Tam exhaled, the faintest noise the only clue that he was present at all. He'd moved as quietly as a vampire and almost as fast, and when I looked more closely at him, I saw that he carried a long instrument in his hand. Not a wand, but a sharpened stick made of a dark wood that must be a weapon. Otherwise, he wore jeans and a shirt as if he'd never undressed at all. Had he expected an attack?

"Can you see anything?" I breathed.

He shook his head, keeping his gaze on the forest below. The impenetrable darkness beyond the trees might hide anything, and one small light wouldn't cut it. I'd need to get closer to stand a chance of seeing beyond the forest's boundary.

Turning away from the window, I made for the stairs.

I expected Tam to object, but he cast one sweeping glance towards the doors of the others' rooms before treading after me.

"Best not to wake them," he whispered, his breath tickling my ear. I shivered, not entirely due to the cold, and shifted the hovering light in front of me so I didn't trip.

Tam walked close behind me as we headed downstairs. I hadn't intended to bring him along for the ride, but I couldn't deny that it was a relief not to be alone against this unknown threat. When we reached the floor below, I made for the window and returned my attention to the mass of trees.

Even one floor below, it was hard to make out any details. The storm raged on, the wind causing the trees to sway against one another with creaking and moaning noises. That might be all I'd heard, but Tam had reacted, too, and the guy didn't strike me as the type of person to panic over unexplained noises. He carried a weapon too, as if he expected to use it.

As we watched, movement stirred at the very front of the forest, where the darkness appeared more solid than elsewhere. A rumbling growl emanated from within the trees.

I tensed, my wand trembling in my hand, and Tam swore softly. "I can't tell what it is."

"Nor me." The trouble with unknown creatures from the afterworld is that a lot of them were, well, unknown. Impossible to identify until they were quite literally staring you in the face.

The growling rose in volume, and the hairs on my arms all stood on end at the same time. I was glad of the darkness that stopped Tam from seeing my hands shaking. I didn't scare easily, but not knowing what we were up against itched underneath my skin and drove me to raise my wand.

"I can use an illumination charm to reveal what it is," I whispered to Tam. "I'll have to open the window, though."

"Most afterworld creatures hate bright lights," he murmured back. "If it flees, it'll be impossible to track in the darkness."

He had a point there, but how were we supposed to fight something we couldn't see?

"We need to know what we're up against." This might be our only chance to take the creature by surprise. Despite its proximity to the tower, the beast hadn't left the forest. Most likely it'd come to assess us as a potential threat instead, but if one of us opened the front door, then the creature might take it as an invitation to attack.

Tam leaned forward. "You're right. I'll open the window."

I moved to help, lifting the wooden frame so I could point my wand directly at the forest. Focusing on the patch of darkness, I flicked my wand, and the gravel path lit up in a blinding flash.

Brightness pierced the forest, but I resisted screwing up my eyes against the glare. The forest wavered before my eyes, and the growling receded, leaving nothing but trees and drizzle and a cold breeze that struck me to the bone.

As the light dimmed, I opened my eyes more fully, but I couldn't see a thing. The creature had vanished into the surrounding forest, and even my illumination spell couldn't penetrate the black mass of trees in the full darkness.

"Well done," said Maurice from behind me. "Now you've done it."

I spun on my heel, my wand light shining on his pale face. If he'd been standing any closer, I might have punched him in the face. Given the circumstances, it'd have been justifiable.

"What," I asked, "are you doing here?"

How long had he been here? Long enough to figure out what we were doing, evidently, but he'd made no move to offer us a hand or announce his presence.

Tam didn't look surprised to see the vampire. "The beast has gone. Did either of you see what it looked like?"

"No." I glanced at Maurice. "How about you make yourself useful and chase after it? I doubt the beast is faster than you are."

"If I had a death wish, sure."

"You're already dead." I wouldn't have been falling over myself to volunteer in his place, admittedly, but it was true that the vampire was the fastest on the team and the only one of us with a fighting chance of catching our target.

"Congratulations for reading the chapter on 'vampires' in the basic magical handbook."

"Maurice," said Tam in exasperated tones. "I'd appreciate it if you took this situation more seriously. We're lucky the creature didn't take us unawares, but it came to the tower for a reason."

"Probably to find whoever was nosing around the forest," he drawled. "And who trampled all over the site of its summoning."

"The police already went to the scene too." They hadn't seen the markings, though, and the urge arose to demand an explanation for his apparent shock at the sight of them in my mind. He'd begrudgingly apologised to Farley for causing her to pass out, but he hadn't clarified *why* the sight of the ritual had affected him so strongly, and I didn't buy the theory that he was simply shocked that anyone would be cruel enough to cut out someone's heart. No … there was another reason, and the most paranoid part of me wondered if he knew something that he hadn't told the others.

Under Tam's watchful eye, probing him for answers would not be wise, so I held my tongue and shut down the thought in case Maurice picked up on it. The vampire seemed to have stuck to Tam's orders not to invade my privacy again, but the trouble with mind-reading was that it was virtually impossible to prove one way or another. Short of someone reading *his* thoughts, I'd have to trust that his fear of suffering punishment at Tam's hands outweighed his desire to annoy the crap out of me.

In the meantime, I'd keep a tight lid on my thoughts whenever I was around him.

"Exactly," Tam said in response to my comment. "Stanley has been near the scene too, at least once."

True enough. Come to think of it, maybe Maurice's 'death wish' comment had referred to Stanley's gun and not the monster. Vampires weren't immune to bullet wounds, after all. Was Stanley likely to be roaming around at night? If he'd summoned the creature himself, he might think he was safe, but none of the others seemed to think of him as a potential suspect.

Maurice made a sceptical noise. "What were you hoping to gain by casting that spell, anyway? Were you trying to blind your target?"

"I wanted to get a look at what we were up against," I told him. "It didn't seem keen to leave the forest, but I didn't want to risk it getting into the tower if I opened the door and went outside to look up close."

"Really?" A smirk appeared on his face. "Whatever happened to Perry the awe-inspiring monster hunter? I'd have thought you'd be dying to prove you live up to your reputation."

"All right, genius, tell me what you'd have done in my place." I propped a hand on my hip. "Should we have stayed in bed and waited for it to go away? Would you have bothered getting up at all if you hadn't heard Tam and me outside in the corridor?"

He bared his fangs, which retracted when Tam shot him a warning look. "That's enough. I'll wake the others. You two can go back to bed or stay down here, it's your choice—but remember what I said to you earlier. Especially you, Maurice."

He turned towards the stairs, holding the stick-like object in his hands. It looked a bit like a stake from this angle, which might explain why Maurice slunk away into the living room without another word.

I didn't trust myself not to punch the vampire in the nose if I stayed downstairs, so I went up to my room to get properly dressed. If our altercation was a preview of how our team would fare in a real battle, it didn't bode well for when we came face to face with the monster in person. As I tugged on my clothes, I heard Tam waking Farley and Callum to tell them the unwelcome news. I figured I'd better give the former a wide berth until I got my emotions under control, trusting Tam to explain the situation calmly. He hadn't seemed scared of the creature at all, and despite the tension simmering in the air, Farley didn't look any more rattled than Callum did when the two of them left their rooms.

As I joined them, I could see how Tam had become a team leader because he had the situation firmly in hand, answering everyone's questions in the same calm manner. He even got the fire going again while the rest of us huddled in blankets to keep out the chill. Maurice, who of course couldn't feel the cold, sat in the farthest seat from the fireplace and ignored everyone else's questions.

"Why'd it choose now to come to the tower?" asked Callum. "The creature was summoned on Saturday morning, right?"

"If I had to guess, it knew we found the site of the ritual yesterday." Maurice, unfortunately, had probably guessed that one right. "It came to check out its adversaries."

Farley twisted around in her seat. "It saw you?"

"I don't know. It didn't leave the woods even when I used an illumination charm."

Maurice stirred. "Is nobody going to comment on one of us breaking the no-magic-in-the-tower rule?"

"It doesn't count when there's a monster outside the doors," said Tam. "You know that."

"Even *I* know that," said Farley. "And I don't even use a wand most of the time. They don't agree with me."

Reading between the lines, I assumed her reasons had to do with her empath abilities, but that didn't entirely account for her reaction when I'd pulled out my wand on my first day. It might be that someone else's emotions had prompted her response instead, but whose? Maurice's?

"The creature wasn't close enough to the tower for us

to see it properly," said Tam. "It fled at once. That suggests it didn't want to fight, or it thought it wouldn't stand a chance against all of us at the same time."

"Only two of us were up there," I commented. "Well, three, but Maurice didn't show his face until after it'd gone."

Maurice narrowed his eyes, but he couldn't dispute my claim when it was the truth.

"It's more likely that it wanted to check out whether we're a threat," said Callum. "Unless it came in search of prey."

I wrapped the blanket tighter around my cold arms. "If it's the latter, then Stanley is a more obvious target, being right in front of its nose."

Tam glanced at me. "Stanley's house is protected with spells. So is the tower, in fact."

"Is it?" I hadn't asked, though it seemed obvious in retrospect. Most of the Wardens' secure bases were laden with security spells in case one of their prisoners went on the rampage. "Then ... was it trying to lure us outside?"

"There's a possibility that it was, yes," said Tam. "Which unfortunately means it might still be looking for prey."

Nobody spoke for a moment. The police must have warned everyone in the village not to go outside, but there wasn't a great deal of choice in prey for a beast living in an isolated forest like this one. Just Stanley, the other people of Hexworth ... and us.

"It'll be dawn soon," Farley ventured. "If the creature doesn't like the sunlight, then it might go into hiding during the day."

"I doubt it's the sunlight that's a problem," Maurice

said. "Perry blasted it with the equivalent of a nuclear flare. Anyone would hide their eyes from that. Doesn't mean it's scared of the sun."

"I really don't know what else you expected me to do," I said. "It's a beast from the afterworld. They're almost always nocturnal, so Farley's right, and it might have a lair it hides in during the day."

Like vampires, except that creature had never been human, and the afterworld was inaccessible to anyone except via a branch of magic more likely to kill the user than not.

Nobody else offered a comment, and the minutes crept by as we waited for dawn to paint grey fingers along the carpet from the window. Callum eventually dozed off again, which I envied, but Farley remained wide awake, the same as me. Maurice sat like a statue, but Tam was equally still, his hands wrapped around that stake-like instrument.

When his phone rang, everyone jumped, and Callum woke up with a jolt. Tam himself went outside into the corridor to answer it and returned within minutes.

"There's been another attack," he said. "Near Hexworth. We were right ... the beast was searching for prey."

And by the grave note in Tam's voice, it'd found exactly what it was looking for.

9

A moment of silence passed amid our group as we took in Tam's grave pronouncement.

"Someone else was attacked?" Callum asked. "You mean killed?"

"Janessa didn't say, but it doesn't sound promising," said Tam. "The victim was taking a dawn walk, apparently, and the creature attacked him without warning."

"Not in the forest?"

"No, but nearby," he said. "I'll have to ask Janessa for more details in person."

I glanced out the window, where dawn had barely advanced into proper daylight. "It can't have happened long ago, then."

"The police showed up at once when neighbours heard the screaming," he said. "They were already too late."

Chills raced down my arms. This wasn't like the first death. Sacrifice or not, the perpetrator had been human. The second death hit a different note, and if the monster had selected the townspeople as its prey, then the pressure was on us to get a handle on the situation before anyone else fell victim to its hunger.

"Do you think we should shortcut through the woods?" I asked. "The monster might still be lurking near the village, waiting to take someone unawares."

"I don't think that's advisable," said Tam. "We already know it has no intention of attacking all of us at once, so it's likely to avoid a direct confrontation. When we hunt it down, we need to be cautious, and we need to know what we're up against."

No kidding. If we'd been able to get a proper look at the beast earlier, we might have been better prepared, but the creature now knew more about us than the other way around. Enough that it'd opted to seek out its prey elsewhere, and now a second person was dead.

The truth sat hollowly inside my chest as we left the tower, taking the longer route to the village instead of the paths through the forest. If the police had heard the screaming, then surely Stanley had, too, but he hadn't come to the rescue of his fellow villager. Perhaps he'd hidden inside his house out of self-preservation, but if he'd heard anything in the woods last night, he might have valuable information to share. Not that he'd share it with me, but perhaps the police or one of the others would have better luck getting through to him.

Of course, first I'd have to actually convince them that he was a potential suspect.

Nobody said much as we walked. Even Callum's expression was grim, while Maurice kept yawning. This was usually the time he went to bed, no doubt, but perhaps he hadn't wanted to stay alone at the tower when the rest of us weren't around. Though it was more likely that he just wanted to know what was going on. He wasn't the only one.

When we reached the cobbled street leading through the centre of Hexworth, Tam turned to address the rest of us. "I'll talk to Janessa myself and find out everything I can about the attack and the victim. One of you should come with me—Farley?"

"Sure," she said. "And—the others?"

Tam met my eyes briefly. "The attack happened near the forest border. I want you three to look around the area—*only* the immediate area, and not any farther into the forest. Unless, that is, you see any signs of the beast. Then you're to take the course of action you deem best, within the boundaries of our rules. Does that sound fair?"

We were allowed to fight? I supposed we'd have little choice if the creature was breathing down our necks. "Sure."

"Three of us should be able to take it on," said Callum, though he didn't sound entirely certain. "I doubt it'll pick a fight with all of us at the same time, though."

Maurice grunted, no doubt displeased at being placed in the same group as me. Tam must have faith in us not to get into another fight, but I could understand why he'd asked Farley to accompany him to the police station alone. There was less chance of her running headfirst into strong emotions since the police had already seen the scene of the crime for themselves.

Even so, I really didn't want to go monster-hunting with Maurice, not when I had little doubt that he wouldn't hesitate to throw me into the path of the monster to save his own skin. To be honest, the feeling was mutual, so Callum would have to play mediator between us. He let Maurice take the lead down the winding street, while I followed with my hands in my pockets and my instincts on full alert. Eerie silence blanketed the stone houses on either side, with curtains drawn across windows and doors locked and bolted.

Soon we came to the road's end where the low wall around the outskirts of the town bordered on the edges of the forest.

"Here we are." Callum took in a deep breath as if to steady himself to face whatever we might find. "We're not supposed to walk any farther than the wall, but I assume Tam wants us to take stock of any clues the attacker left behind."

And if it's still around. The forest appeared as impenetrable as ever, but we didn't need to look far to see the carnage. Even the ongoing rain hadn't washed away the bloodstains on the stone wall, while the mud had been churned up as if the victim had been dragged into the forest. By what, though? I didn't see any footprints, human or otherwise, but deep gouges in the mud like holes left by fence posts had filled with rainwater. Those hadn't been there the day before.

The coppery smell of blood hung in the air, but when Callum sniffed, he shook his head. "I still don't smell a predator."

I tilted my head, peering at the ground. "I don't see any footprints, either, but those gouges weren't there yesterday, were they?"

I crouched beside the wall. The ground was marked as if someone had dug a sharp stick into the mud and dragged it into the woods alongside the unfortunate hiker.

"No." Callum's voice sounded unsteady. "You okay, Maurice?"

"Obviously." His voice came from farther off than I expected, and when I dragged my gaze away from the wall, I saw that he'd backed up a few steps. When he caught me looking, he scowled and muttered, "The blood is setting off my vampire instincts."

"Oh, great." I'd forgotten the smell of blood would test his control over his urge to sink his fangs into the nearest warm-blooded human. "Keep your distance from the rest of us, then."

"I'm not going to bite anyone." He approached the wall farther down and climbed over in a swift bound. "I'll look around here."

"I thought Tam said not to go into the—" I broke off when he vanished. "Forest. Well, it's his own fault if he's next."

"He's fast enough to outrun any threat," Callum said.

"True, but if he runs back this way, he might bring the monster on his tail." It seemed the imminent threat of another warning wasn't enough to deter him from skirting the rules. He was like one of those delinquent teens who were forever in detention ... which I'd know about because I'd been one of them myself. "Well, if he does, it's his funeral as well as the monster's."

His brow crinkled. "Didn't we already decide the beast was nocturnal?"

"So's our fanged friend, yet here we are." I returned my attention to the crime scene. "What do you think happened here, then?"

"The monster grabbed his victim, dragged him into

the woods, and then…" He gestured at the mess on the other side of the wall.

"Ripped out his heart and devoured it," I guessed. "I suppose whoever summoned him gave him a taste for vital organs."

It made me queasy to think about, but I forced myself to ignore the grim image and focused on the questions stirring in the back of my mind. The gouge-like markings on the ground didn't resemble the prints of any creature I was aware of, but it couldn't have left no traces at all, surely.

Callum reached into his pocket for his phone. "I'll get a picture of the scene to show Tam. He might be able to find clues we didn't see ourselves."

"Good call." I paced the scene while he snapped a few pictures and then climbed over the wall myself. The gouge-like markings merged into a trail of churned-up mud, but the rain had turned the path into a swamp and made it impossible to track a definite route.

Did Maurice know where he was going? You'd think he'd be back by now, but perhaps he'd found a clue … or perhaps he'd had another reason altogether for going into the woods.

Unbidden, my mind strayed back to his reaction yesterday when I'd revealed the markings my spell had exposed. There were a dozen possible explanations for his shock, but I couldn't deny the possibility that the person who'd used the ritual had left the evidence out in the open because they thought they were safe from ever getting caught. They hadn't known someone would use a spell to expose their handiwork.

It would ruin all the goodwill I'd built with the rest of

the team if I accused one of them of murder, and besides, I didn't know if vampires could even use that sort of magic. Even the ones who'd previously been witches or wizards found it hard to use a wand after they awoke as one of the undead, though their new abilities more than made up for it. Unless he was working with someone else who *did* have access to a wand, Maurice likely wasn't the culprit we were looking for.

Hoping Callum hadn't guessed the direction of my thoughts, I returned my attention to the scene. "I wonder why it waited over a day before attacking someone. The first victim was stabbed to death by the person who sacrificed him, not by the creature itself, so this is the first time it's killed."

He grimaced. "Maybe it wasn't hungry yet."

"I don't know…" I stiffened at the sound of a branch snapping underfoot. *Someone else is here.* Not Maurice. The sound belonged to someone wearing heavy boots, and sure enough, I spotted none other than Stanley approaching the low wall. He carried his gun, though he didn't point it at any of us this time, and he levelled me with a glare.

"I told you not to come in here," he growled. "This is your fault. This man's blood is on your hands."

I raised my hands. "Hey, I didn't do anything."

Did he know we'd scared the creature away from the tower the previous night? Even if he did, that didn't lessen my suspicion towards him. The creature would certainly have passed his house on its way to find its prey, but it hadn't targeted him. *If he's trying to deflect the blame from himself, it won't work.*

"You provoked that creature by wandering around the

woods," he growled. "Don't think I didn't hear you yesterday, even after I warned you to stay away."

"Our whole team was there." Four of us, anyway, but why single me out? "Besides, you can't expect us to ignore some unknown monster attacking the locals. I wasn't even in town when it first showed up, but *you* were."

"You have no idea what you're talking about."

"Don't I?" I met his steely gaze with a challenge. "I know you have defences on your house, but you can't deny it looks suspicious that the creature didn't attack you when you live directly in the middle of its hunting grounds."

"You've been snooping around my house, have you?"

"No, my teammates told me."

"Your teammates." He gave a short laugh. "You still think you belong among them? You're deluding yourself."

Okay, that was uncalled for.

"That's enough," Callum said. "Stanley, you might not like it, but we're neighbours. We're here to help find the creature and kill it if necessary."

"You won't be able to kill it," he growled. "It's from the other side. They don't die easily."

"And just how do you know that?" I queried, unable to resist it. "Speaking from personal experience, are you?"

"Don't they teach you anything at the academy anymore?" He scoffed. "I suppose a mouthy witch like you never paid attention in class."

"No need for the personal comments." I'd dropped out of school, sure, but it was none of his business. He didn't know the first thing about me. "I came here to get rid of this creature. I didn't bring it with me."

His eyes narrowed. "You made the situation worse by barging into the investigation. Now someone else is dead."

"Made it worse? How, exactly?" He couldn't possibly think a predator would have refrained from going after the villagers if I hadn't been around, surely. "If you know anything more, then I think the police would appreciate it if you told them."

Instead of replying, he turned and walked away into the woods, his boots leaving a thick trail behind him.

"He has some nerve accusing *me* of trampling on crime scenes. Look at that." I gestured at the mess he'd left in his wake. "What *is* his problem?"

"You." Maurice had reappeared, silent as usual. "I don't know why you're surprised."

"How long have you been lurking there?" I'd had about enough of *his* attitude as well. "You know, I think we should send the police to pay him a visit. He expects us to believe his claims that it's a coincidence that he was able to avoid getting attacked by the monster when it's roaming around outside his door?"

"It's from the afterworld," Maurice said. "I guess he's right and you skipped that class at school."

"I know how the afterworld works. It doesn't make that dude immune to being disembowelled." Or having his heart ripped out. Whichever.

"How have you lasted this long in the job without knowing the basics?" said Maurice. "A handful of sage can keep the dead from touching him. He probably has some in his pockets as well as outside his house."

"I'm aware of that." Sage repelled most spirits as well as their distant relations, but Stanley's lack of concern that he'd be a target remained suspicious in my eyes. "If I were him, I wouldn't bet my safety on a handful of herbs that can easily be dropped or washed away in the rain. Did you check out his house when you were roaming the forest just then?"

"Unlike some people, I know better than to break into people's houses."

"Meaning you can't get in without an invitation." One of the few downsides to being a vampire. When he scowled, I added, "It was a joke. Besides, you don't need to break *into* his house to look at the defences outside."

"Still," said Callum, "I wouldn't want to get on Stanley's bad side, personally."

"Bit late now," I said. "I'm not advocating that we walk over there and break the door down, but there aren't many people on the suspect list for who might have summoned that creature, and right now, he's at the top of mine. He lives right there in the forest, he admitted to being able to protect himself from the creature while it attacks his fellow villagers, and he's acting as if *we're* the bigger threat."

"You, not we," Maurice corrected. "He thinks you're a safety risk, which is true."

"I'm not the one ripping out people's hearts. Does he really think a bit of sage will keep him safe from that?" If I were him, I'd have legged it the day of the first attack. "If I know one thing about summoning rituals, it's that most people who meddle with the afterworld have no idea what they'll find when they contact the other side. It's like a game of Russian Roulette where literally anything might show up and bite your face off."

As to why they would summon a beast from the realm of the dead to begin with, the answers varied depending on the circumstances. Sometimes the person responsible was hoping to reach a dead loved one on the other side. On other occasions, it was power they wanted. I didn't yet know which applied to Stanley, but whatever my teammates claimed, he fit the profile of the summoner exactly.

As for Maurice? He'd offered no explanation as to what he'd been doing in the forest himself, and neither had he mentioned finding any clues. He hadn't been the one who'd driven Stanley in our direction too, had he? I hastily shoved a wall in the way of that question before the vampire plucked it from my thoughts. If Stanley was guilty, it didn't automatically make the vampire innocent, though.

Callum shook his head. "Enough speculating. We'll go and meet Tam and see what he has to say."

10

Callum, Maurice, and I left the woods behind and walked back to the police station to meet Tam. The walk took less than ten minutes, which reminded me how close to the rest of the village's inhabitants the attack had taken place. No wonder the streets were so quiet. Everyone with any sense was hiding away until they felt safe to come outside.

It might take a while at this rate. I had two suspects but zero proof, while our team dynamic was on shaky ground. But for everyone's sake, we had to get rid of the monster *and* ensure its summoner ended up behind bars where they belonged. No pressure.

Callum led the way to the police station. Through the glass door, I spotted Tam near the desk, talking to Janessa and one of her scowling subordinates. Nearby, Farley waved and beckoned for us to come in.

Janessa tutted when the three of us attempted to crowd into the already pocket-sized office. "Back already?"

"What did you find?" asked Tam. "Did something else happen?"

Yes, we met a certain unfriendly local, and our resident vamp got a bit too overexcited about all the blood. Also, one of them is probably the culprit. I surreptitiously cast a look at the vampire, but he didn't react as if he'd heard my silent response.

"No, but we looked around the area," Callum replied aloud. "There weren't any strange scents or footprints, but there were some strange markings on the ground. I think they were left by the creature, but they don't look like any I'm familiar with. I didn't detect the scent of a predator, either, which is odd."

"Something killed a man," Janessa said sourly. "Unless you're claiming that an invisible ghost was responsible for ripping his heart out."

For the afterworld, that wasn't *entirely* unheard of, but her dismissive tone made it clear she wouldn't believe any of our theories until we brought cold, hard evidence. As for a certain forest-dwelling local...

"Not a ghost," I put in. "A flesh-and-blood creature summoned with the aid of a human, who committed the first murder."

"Which left no footprints, allegedly," said the officer. "I'm not buying it."

There *were* footprints around the scene now, thanks to Stanley, but pointing that out would probably lead them to pin the blame on us for not stopping him. If in doubt, blame the outsider. *I see how it is.*

"It left markings," said Callum. "I can compare the photos with our resources back at the tower to see if they match anything the Wardens have dealt with before."

"Exactly," Tam said to Janessa. "I don't think there's anything we can do for the victim at this point, but I offer my condolences."

"Easy for you to say." She sniffed. "Never seen anything like it in all my years of running this department. Invisible beasts indeed. And you say it came to your tower, did you?"

"Yes, but it fled as soon as we tried to get a closer look," said Tam. "It seems to favour lone victims. I'd advise the locals to stay indoors at night and to avoid going near the forest at all until it's caught."

"Don't tell me how to do my job," said Janessa. "We already gave that advice to the townspeople, but they'll do as they like. They like their freedom."

I'm sure they do, but that creature also likes the taste of their vital organs.

"Regardless, I'll get in touch when we have another update." Tam turned towards the door, prompting Callum to lead the way out ahead of Farley and me. Maurice hadn't even come in, instead lurking outside in a typical vampire-like manner.

Tam was the last to leave the police station. "Did you see anyone else at the scene of the attack?"

"Yes," I said at once. "Stanley came trampling through the crime scene and left muddy footprints everywhere, so it'll serve him right if he gets arrested as a suspect."

Concern flickered within his gaze. "He didn't give you any trouble, did he?"

"Well, he didn't point his gun directly at my face this time, so I'd say it was an improvement," I said. "Otherwise, he decided we were somehow to blame for the monster's attack."

"Technically he blamed you, not the rest of us," Maurice corrected.

"For going near the site of the ritual," I added for Tam's benefit. "He also seemed to think that we haven't a hope of killing the beast ourselves, which seems an interesting perspective from an innocent bystander."

Maurice gave a snort. "Yeah, I'm sure accusing him of committing the crime is going to help."

"I didn't accuse him of anything." I turned away from the vampire. "I did mention that it was suspicious that he'd managed to avoid being attacked when his house is right on top of the monster's hunting grounds. He also seemed pretty knowledgeable on the subject of beasts from the afterworld."

Tam grimaced. "You aren't wrong, but he's lived here a long time. No doubt his house is well-equipped to keep out any potential attackers, but that doesn't erase the danger to his own safety if he continues to wander around the woods."

"He implied that carrying a handful of sage in his pocket makes him immune," I added. "I don't think it's a bad idea for the police to pay him a visit—or vice versa, if they want to avoid the forest—and ask him some questions."

"I doubt any of us would be able to convince him to volunteer himself for questioning, and the police will certainly be avoiding the forest for the time being," Tam said. "For the record, I don't think Stanley's the culprit, though. He's pretty much a fixture here in Hexworth, however unfriendly he might be."

"I agree," Callum said. "He shouldn't have spoken to you the way he did, though. As for the beast ... I freely admit I don't have a ton of experience with monsters from the afterworld. Do they usually leave no scent?"

"It's not unheard of," I said. "The markings it left, though … they don't match anything I'm familiar with. They don't really look like footprints at all either."

"I'll come and have a look myself," Tam said. "It might be worth knocking on a few doors to find out if anyone living nearby got a glimpse of the creature."

"I assume they'd have already reported it to the police if they did," Farley said. "Everyone who wasn't sleeping with earplugs in would have heard the noise too."

"True," said Tam. "We can't talk to everyone in town, so we'll need to be strategic about this."

"Yeah, and some of them will be pretty freaked out," added Callum, with a brief glance at Farley. "Which might be an issue."

Farley cleared her throat. "After being around you lot all morning, I can handle it."

And that was that. As we left the police station behind, Tam fell into step with me. "Did Stanley go back home after you left the forest?"

"I assume so, but who knows," I said. "Why, do you want to talk to him?"

"The thought crossed my mind," he said. "I might have to do so alone, though."

"Wise idea since he's decided I'm a troublemaker." Which might be true, but he didn't know the first thing about me. "He acted as if I'm the reason that guy got attacked when I wasn't even here when the ritual took place. You have to admit that if he's worried that I'm going to expose him as a criminal, his attitude makes much more sense, doesn't it?"

His brow furrowed. "I don't know, Perry. Like I said, he's lived here for years. There's no reason for him to have started performing human sacrifices without any prior signs."

"Does he know someone who died recently?" I asked.

"Not that I'm aware of."

"Why?" asked Callum, overhearing.

"That's one reason people sometimes get into death magic," I elaborated. "They're trying to bring someone back from the other side, and they don't realise that there's no way to be sure that you reach the right target. Once you open a path to the afterworld, anything might answer."

"Sounds like you have personal experience," Maurice remarked.

My jaw twitched. "I've worked on a lot of cases. Nothing exactly like this one, but it's basic information you learn in training."

I wasn't lying, but Maurice's words hit a nerve, and one I'd keep behind a tightly locked wall as long as I was around him. Regardless, nothing in my own history was the slightest bit relevant to this case.

As we neared Reynard's house, Tam slowed his pace. "I wonder if it's worth talking to Reynard again."

"Might be," I remarked. "What about the guy we found role-playing in the woods yesterday?"

"Karl?" said Tam. "I confirmed with the police that he was at a convention over the weekend and didn't get back until late Sunday, so it's plausible for him to have not heard about the first attack until we told him yesterday. I think he's grasped that it's a good idea to avoid the woods for the time being."

"Reynard, though?" I ventured. "He's the one who's already got into trouble with the police…"

"Exactly." Tam turned to Callum and the others. "Perry and I will talk to him and then go to the crime scene. Can you three go ahead and knock on some other doors near the scene and ask if anyone saw the creature?"

"Sure," said Callum easily.

Maurice simply grunted. He should be fast asleep by this hour, which might explain his mood, but that was no excuse for his constant belittling comments. No doubt that was partly why Tam had asked me to come with him instead of joining the vampire's group again. Though it was a risk to put the mind-reader and the empath on the same team, Maurice and Farley did at least seem to get along with one another.

"That okay with you?" Tam addressed me.

"Of course." Probably I was overthinking the matter, but Maurice's biting comments alongside Stanley's claims that I'd made the situation worse for everyone had wormed their way under my skin despite my best efforts. "Let's talk to Reynard."

I wondered belatedly how his interview with the police had gone the previous day, and if they'd come sniffing around his potion collection again. No doubt they had more important things on their minds—like the monster stalking the village's outskirts.

Tam took the lead and knocked on his door, but no response came. It took three more knocks before Reynard appeared in the doorway, dishevelled and wearing the same dressing gown as he had the day before. A bright-orange substance stained his hands and sleeves, and a whiff of herbs accompanied his presence.

"What?" he grumbled. "Can't a person sleep in these days?"

"We wondered if you heard the noise outside last night," said Tam. "Near the forest."

"Hard to miss," he said. "It woke me up at the crack of dawn. I was up until midnight, so I didn't appreciate being disturbed."

"Someone was being murdered," I informed him. "We're looking for witnesses."

"Witness?" He looked blearily at me. "Hardly. I sleep in the basement."

Okay... "You spoke to the police yesterday, didn't you?"

"They keep on about those bloody potions," he muttered. "Can't do anything these days, can you?"

"They're illegal," Tam said in stern tones. "Is there anything else you want to tell us?"

"No." He retreated into the house, and the door swung closed behind him.

Bewildered, I turned towards Tam. "That was instructive. He wasn't exactly sympathetic towards the poor victim, was he?"

"I don't think he knows how serious it was yet."

"He didn't give us the chance to explain anything either." I gave the house a last searching look before walking away. "Is he the sort who might be into creepy ritualistic sacrifices, do you think?"

"I would have said no, but he has a lax relationship with the law, to say the least." Tam fell into step with me. "Let's have a look around the scene."

"All right." Mentally adding Reynard back to the suspect list, I walked with him back to the wall overlooking the forest.

Tam sucked in a breath at the sight of the bloodstains. His hand strayed to his weapons belt, where he wore the stick-like instrument he'd been carrying earlier. In daylight, it resembled a sharpened branch, tapered to a knife's edge. Interesting choice of weapon, but he moved as if he knew how to use it.

"Strange," Tam murmured. "I see what you mean about there not being any traces."

"Yeah." I pointed down at the gouge-like markings in the soil. "That's the closest to footprints or tracks we found."

In fact, now that I had a comparison point, they looked a little like they'd been made by a branch or a sharpened post … which made no sense. I'd heard of monsters with hooves, like satyrs, but I'd never heard of a creature with pointy branches for feet. Weird.

My imagination conjured a dozen possible monsters, each more unlikely than the next, while Tam walked along the wall and then examined the scene from the other side. Eventually, I caught sight of Maurice lurking apart from the others, not volunteering to knock on any doors. If I'd heard a vicious murder outside my house, the last thing I'd want would be a visit from a grumpy vampire, so I opted not to tell tales on him.

When Tam finished checking the crime scene, we met up with the others at the end of the road.

"Any luck?" he asked.

"No," Callum said. "Everyone heard the noise, but I couldn't find anyone who looked out the window at the time of the attack. I think most people went into hiding as soon as they heard screaming."

I couldn't say I blamed them in the slightest. We'd

pretty much done the same when we'd stayed in the tower instead of pursuing the creature into the forest, but now that it had the townspeople in its sights, the idea of leaving them to their fate was out of the question.

Tam inclined his head. "I think we've done all we can here. Short of combing the entire wood—and the creature might be hiding during the day—our best option is to check our records to identify the creature so we can make a plan to entrap and destroy it."

"Can we identify it?" Maurice sounded dubious. "According to our new team member, the beast could be literally anything."

All eyes turned towards me. "We can rule out a fair few otherworldly beasts based on the lack of footprints or scent, among other things. Do you have a guidebook or anything back at the tower?"

"We do." Tam began to lead the way down the path through the middle of the village. "We don't have a guide specifically for beasts from the afterworld, though. It's illegal to gather that information in case it falls into the wrong hands. Our guides mostly cover the common monsters of the magical world, but that's not what we're dealing with here."

"In other words, we don't have anything," Maurice said. "We're going in without any knowledge of what we're up against."

"We're not going into anything," said Tam. "We might not have official guidebooks on that particular branch of creature, but the Wardens' offices will have that information."

"Wish we had it ourselves." I could understand why they wouldn't want guidebooks on how to summon the dead floating around, but we needed to be able to do our jobs. "I can ask Kellen..."

"That was the plan," said Tam. "If all else fails, we have a general plan to deal with beasts from the afterworld, and we can adapt it if it doesn't work out."

"That's a fairly significant 'if,'" Maurice said around a yawn. The daylight must be getting to him. Some stories said vampires burst into flames in sunlight, but they just got sleepy instead. Pity, because it would have been an improvement if he'd had to stay in the tower to avoid catching on fire.

I pushed that thought out of my mind, but Maurice didn't seem to have overheard this time. He kept yawning as we left the village behind us and walked uphill towards the tower. I wouldn't have minded a nap myself. The fact that the creature was likely nocturnal meant this might be our last chance to catch up on sleep, but nightfall would roll around before we knew it.

And then? If last night's victim hadn't satisfied its hunger, then it might go looking for new prey.

When we got back to the tower, the first thing Tam did was make everyone coffee and have us share out the tasks for preparing breakfast. Then we started compiling our knowledge.

Callum showed Farley the photos of the odd markings we'd seen at the scene of the attack since she was the only person who hadn't seen them up close. At the sight of them, she blinked in confusion. "What made those marks? Really sharp claws?"

"Possibly," said Callum. "Like a gargoyle shifter."

"But it's not winged," I added. "If it could fly, it'd have gone farther from the forest to find its prey."

"It can move fast, though." Farley lowered her gaze. "Given how quickly it got from one side of the forest to the other."

"The forest isn't that big, though," I pointed out. "It was dark, true, but most afterworld creatures have strong night vision."

Tam placed a notebook on the table. "Perry, do you think you can draw those symbols you saw at the ritual site from memory?"

"I don't think so." When a hint of disappointment entered his expression, I added, "They were kind of … indistinct. I'm not sure if they show up on camera, but I wish I'd snapped a picture when I had the chance."

"We'll come back to that later, then," Tam said.

I could see where this was going. If all else failed, the odds were high that we'd need to make another trip into the forest by nightfall.

11

As I'd anticipated, we soon hit a wall with our research. The collection of books in the living room did contain several guidebooks to common magical monsters but not beasts from the afterworld. I found a few references to ghosts or poltergeists, but the instructions for dealing with them amounted to 'put sage around your house and wait for it to go away.' Not an option in our current situation.

"Really, it ought to be possible to write a guide to identifying afterworld monsters without including instructions on how to summon one," I grouched, helping Callum put the unhelpful textbooks back on the shelves. "You'd think a past Warden would have compiled a guide like they have for pretty much every other magical monster."

"I'm sure they have," he said. "The Wardens' management keeps people from sharing those records widely, but Tam will be able to get them from Kellen, no problem."

I hoped he was right because the alternative was

waiting for nightfall and combing the forest for the monster's lair ourselves. Thanks to the storm, the sky was already gloomy and dull despite being mid-afternoon, which didn't help my growing sleepiness.

Luckily for all of us, Maurice had gone to bed instead of staying downstairs and making a nuisance of himself. Farley had dozed off right there in an armchair, while Tam had gone downstairs to the training room an hour ago, perhaps to delve into the case records he kept locked in his desk. That left Callum and me to put together our knowledge, which didn't amount to much.

"Haven't you dealt with similar cases in the past?" I asked him.

"No two cases are identical." He glanced over at Farley's sleeping form. "This seems like a case involving a creature with a corporeal form, not a spirit."

"Any creature from the afterworld can be banished by a Reaper," I commented. "Too bad we don't have one of those on standby."

Callum raised a brow. "Have you ever met a Reaper?"

"No. They're loners, for the most part." They also worked for a council even more secretive than our own and were only accountable to fellow Reapers. "I'm sure the Wardens' office has a Reaper's contact details, but it's anyone's guess as to how long it'd take for one to get here before the creature strikes again."

Callum gave a shudder. "Weird. It's not a ghost we're dealing with, I'm sure, but I wonder why you and Tam couldn't see it last night."

"It must have been hiding." I'd seen nothing solid but trees, but something far more solid and dangerous than a ghost had stabbed that man to death and ripped out his heart. "In the forest."

"Perry." Tam had returned to the living room, accompanied by the strong scent of potion ingredients. The source, a basket full of small bags of herbs, he carried in one hand. "Callum, Farley, can you help me put this sage around the tower?"

"Sure." I left the bookshelves and took a bag of sage from the basket. "At least we can rely on a tried-and-true way to repel beasts from the afterworld, even if we don't know which we're dealing with."

Callum took one too. "Farley's out for the count. To tell you the truth, I might need to join her later."

"Go ahead," Tam said. "Maurice is already asleep, and we're better off coming back to the case when we're all refreshed."

True, but I couldn't help feeling that we'd made little progress since our return to the tower. "Have you heard from Kellen yet?"

"He said the description of those markings we found doesn't sound familiar, but he'll ask around the department to see if anyone else knows."

"All right." That would have to do for now.

In the meantime, Callum and I helped Tam sprinkle the sage around the outskirts of the tower. It was a simple job, if a tedious one, and Callum took pity on me towards the end when he spotted me yawning every other minute.

"I'll take over from you." He held out a hand for the bag of sage. "You go and have a nap before you keel over."

"Cheers."

I went back to my room and pretty much passed out

on the bed for an hour, after which I awoke to someone rapping on my door.

"Come in." I instantly regretted the words when I caught sight of my dishevelled reflection in the mirror at the same moment Tam walked in. I dragged my fingers through my hair, hoping I hadn't drooled anywhere.

"Hey," said Tam. "Sorry I woke you up, but we don't have much longer before sunset. If we want to go back into the woods before it's dark, now's our last chance."

My tired brain struggled to make sense of his words. "Just us two? Or do you want to wake the others?"

"Maurice needs the sleep more than the rest of us," he said. "Farley … I don't think she wants to go back to the scene of the attack, and I think she'll feel more secure if Callum stays in the tower as well. As for you, I thought we could take a photo of those ritualistic markings you saw and send it to Kellen so he can show it to the wizards and witches in the department. That should narrow down the list of which creature is likely to have answered the summoner."

"Good idea." I pushed to my feet. "Give me five minutes, and I'll join you downstairs."

I'd fallen asleep fully clothed, so I only had to grab my coat and shoes before leaving my room. When I reached the floor below, the distinct sound of someone rapping on the front door drifted upwards.

"Expecting any visitors?" I asked Tam, who shook his head.

"Strange." He climbed downstairs ahead of me. "Maybe a local came to check on us."

I pulled out my wand all the same as we descended. At the foot of the stairs, Tam opened the door, revealing none other than Karl the role-player standing on the gravel path, mercifully without his armour and cardboard sword this time around. I almost didn't recognise him without his props, dressed in ordinary jeans and a jacket with his dark hair in a windswept tangle.

"Karl?" Tam's wariness became surprise. "What are you doing here?"

Karl spoke in a hushed voice. "Someone else from the village was attacked. I don't know if you heard."

He has to be joking. Right? "I'm pretty sure the entire town knows," I told him. "We've been there ourselves, in fact, to talk to the police."

"Oh." He blinked in apparent surprise. "In that case, I hope they catch the person responsible."

"It's not a person," Tam told him. "There's a beast loose in the woods … you didn't walk through the forest on the way here, did you?"

"It was the fastest route. Shouldn't I have?"

"It's not safe in there." How had he avoided being attacked on his way through? "You're better off taking the road—and I'd hurry up if you want to make it back before sunset."

He nodded. "Yes, I will. Thank you."

He ambled off, while Tam and I exchanged bewildered looks. *How did he get through the woods without any trouble?* The monster might be asleep during the day, but it was a miracle Karl had avoided Stanley and his gun if nothing else. Hadn't we told him yesterday that we'd been hunting the killer? He might have come to warn us for that reason, but part of me was kind of tempted to wake up Farley to ask if she picked up on any other emotions from him.

Karl had already gone, though, and we needed to get a move on ourselves.

"Well, that was weird," I remarked. "How could he assume we hadn't heard about the attack? We'd need to be living under a rock to have missed it."

"He did miss the first death," Tam said, "but he wasn't in town at the time."

"Exactly. He's not all there, is he?" I shook my head. "I can't believe he walked straight through the forest without noticing something was off. Or running into Stanley."

Why check up on us at all? Not everyone was out to get us, I knew, but Karl's unexpected visit made me feel doubly uneasy about leaving the tower behind. The others were safer together, even asleep, so it made no sense for me to worry since we were the ones going out into danger. Tam's sense of responsibility towards the others must be rubbing off on me.

"We should go." Tam stepped out onto the gravel path, and I joined him, my gaze skimming the forest on the other side. I wouldn't lie, the notion of walking back in there knowing what might be hiding in the shadows made my skin crawl.

It wasn't like me to fear the dark, but I suppressed a shudder when Tam and I entered the forest together and the trees' upper branches instantly brought a dark canopy over our heads.

"Maybe we should have come in earlier." Despite the sun being over an hour from setting, the thick trees and their sprawling branches gave the path a twilit feel. "I hope the beast doesn't wake up until after sunset."

"We can turn back if you want." Tam's hand rested on the sharpened stick at his belt. "Kellen might be able to help identify the creature without looking at the ritual itself."

"You don't think he will, though," I guessed. "No, I'll carry on. Just wanted to give you a heads-up that I'm probably going to hex any squirrel that crosses my path."

"I'll keep that in mind." His tone relaxed a little. "We'll watch each other's backs. That's how it works."

I couldn't deny it warmed me a little to think of him trusting me enough to watch his back, and my heart gave a flutter that I couldn't entirely put down to nerves about going into the woods. Nobody had trusted me to watch their back … well, ever. Not that I'd given anyone the chance to, admittedly, but I'd never trusted anyone to do the same for me either.

The two of us walked in silence until we came to the site of the summoning. It seemed to take less time than I remembered, in fact, and I had to wonder if there was a reason the summoner had intentionally picked a spot closer to the tower than to the village. Granted, it was natural for them to have picked a spot as deep in the forest as possible to avoid attention … and away from its sole inhabitant, assuming Stanley wasn't the culprit himself.

If not for Tam, I might have overlooked the clearing altogether. Nature had reclaimed it already, roots sprouting from the churned-up mud and masking the area where the symbols had been etched on the ground.

When I waved my wand and cast a revealing spell, the glyphs shimmered into view. They were fainter than they'd been the last time but still visible, so I pulled out my phone and snapped a couple of photos. Even captured on camera, they might not be visible to non-witches or wizards, but Kellen had a whole team full of experts behind him.

"No signal in here, so I'll have to send the message when we leave the forest," I said to Tam. "How do you remember the route so easily without GPS?"

"I've always had a good sense of direction, that's all," he replied. "We should head back."

"Yeah." A raindrop trickled through the canopy, splashing onto my face, followed by another. "Not this again."

"I'm afraid you'll have to get used to the weather if you decide to stay."

My mouth parted. *If you decide to stay?* When we'd spoken yesterday and agreed to start over, he'd begun acting as if I was already part of the team, and I hadn't realised how much I'd grown used to it. Weird. Come to think of it, Kellen had told me to check in with him after a couple of days, but if I called him now, what would I even say? It was one thing claiming I didn't belong here, but Kellen had assigned me to this particular team for a reason. Except for Maurice, everyone had spent the past day acting as if I'd been here for years, and to be honest, so had I.

Tam gave me a sideways look as we walked, but he didn't ask what was on my mind. Good, because I didn't know if I'd have had it in me to give an honest answer. My thoughts were too confused, and now wasn't the time to sort them out. We had to stay on our guard—

A crunching noise sounded nearby, bringing both of us to a halt.

I spun around on the spot, holding my breath. Tam's

hands moved to his weapons belt, while I scanned the bushes, pinpointing the direction of the movement. I pulled out my wand, but Tam shook his head at me, indicating that he wanted me to approach silently.

Was Stanley lurking around? No, he'd have approached us outright and no doubt given me another reprimand. While Tam moved as silently as a ghost, I couldn't take a step without snapping twigs or snagging my arms on bushes or low-hanging branches. The person —or animal—didn't make another sound, and after several minutes, Tam halted, listening.

"Hear anything?" I murmured.

Tam swore under his breath. "Nobody's here. They've gone."

"Maybe I can lure them out of hiding." I raised my wand, but by this point, I'd lost track of the direction.

"I wouldn't," he said. "There's no sense in drawing attention. It's almost sunset."

True. If our mysterious friend had wanted to attack us, they'd have done so already. It wasn't the monster ... but who else was in here? Karl? No, he'd departed back to the village the long way, while Stanley was not subtle in the least. Perhaps it'd been an animal after all.

Tam and I retraced our steps, stopping occasionally to look around for any signs of trouble. The rain worsened until it was impossible to tell the difference between the sound of raindrops lashing against the branches and our own footsteps. When we reached the forest's boundary, I exhaled, feeling some of the tension dissipate ... but not all of it.

"Someone was in there," I said to Tam. "They didn't want us seeing them."

Either they knew the forest better than we did, or they'd moved too fast to be detected. My gaze travelled over the windows of the tower. Had Maurice been asleep the whole time? Since the others had also been sleeping, it'd be hard to confirm if he'd gone out, but it was beyond me to figure out why he might have been wandering around the woods, keeping tabs on us from a distance.

"I'm starting to doubt it was a person we heard," Tam said.

"Don't you think that monster would have scared most of the wildlife off by now?" One of the early clues pointing to a beast from the afterworld was the sudden departure of the regular animals from the area it was hiding in. Usually, they appeared in cities or towns with plenty of human prey, while it was much harder to search an area this remote. "I bet Maurice has probably already sent the local rodent population into hiding."

Maurice was the one team member who was technically dead ... or undead, anyway. That meant he was closer to the creature than anyone else, in terms of abilities, yet he'd offered us no help whatsoever. I gathered that he was usually lazy and sloppy, but some of his behaviour set off my suspicions in a way that was hard to ignore. Like the way he'd vanished into the forest when we'd been sent to check out the scene of the attack. Granted, he might have just had a look around using his swift vampire speed, but there was another possible explanation.

Such as the possibility that he might have been covering something up.

Stanley was still at the top of my suspect list, and while the others might disagree with me, he was an unquestionable outsider—unlike Maurice. Would Tam ever believe someone on his team would be capable of committing a crime? As the new person, I was the least reliable by default, and I didn't want to ruin our tentatively established trust by voicing my suspicions aloud.

At the tower's doorstep, Tam paused. "I'll wake the others, and you can send the pictures to Kellen. That okay?"

"All right." I drew in a breath. "If he still can't identify the creature, though, what then? What do we do when the sun goes down?"

His expression turned grim. "If the creature comes back? We fight."

12

Back inside the tower, I fired off a message to Kellen with the images of the ritual site attached and sat tight to wait for a reply. I'd postponed our call, but with another facedown with our mysterious assailant potentially on the horizon, the case had to take precedence over my decision about my future.

In the meantime, Tam herded the others back downstairs and into the living room. Maurice wore a scowl that suggested that a nap had not improved his mood in the slightest. Unless, that is, my suspicions that he'd been slinking around the woods instead of sleeping were correct.

"What?" he asked of Tam. "This better be good news."

"Right now, we're waiting for a response from the office," Tam told everyone. "We sent them all the information we have on the creature that we've observed so far."

"That's it?" The vampire cocked a brow. "What was the point in waking me up?"

"It's almost nightfall," Tam said. "If the creature

approaches the tower again, we need to be prepared. I'm hoping the office will send a reply before that eventuality, but if they're unable to identify the creature, then that's on us."

"Otherwise, we have to stay here until it gets someone else?" As Maurice spoke, thunder rumbled in the background, and the rain intensified, pounding against the windowsill.

"Do you think anyone in their right mind would go outside in that?" Farley gestured at the window. "I certainly wouldn't, monster or no monster."

"Hope Karl made it home." For the others' benefit, I added, "Our friendly neighbourhood role-playing guy came to check up on us earlier."

"Why?" Callum asked.

"He assumed we didn't know about the second attack," Tam answered. "We set him right, but he was lucky not to be attacked when he walked through the forest."

"Does that make him a suspect?" Maurice leaned forward in his seat. "He was wandering in the woods with a sword yesterday too."

"The sword was made of cardboard," I reminded him. "Also, there'd be no reason for him to knock on our door and draw attention if he was the culprit we were looking for."

"Exactly," said Tam.

Maurice's mouth turned down at the corners. "So, we have no suspects, no clues about the actual monster, and no way to stop it attacking one of us next."

"We put sage around the entire tower," I said. "Which you'd know if you hadn't been asleep at the time."

"Guys," Farley said. "Simmer down."

Most of the animosity was coming from Maurice, not me, but I wasn't even an empath and his attitude grated on me. It must be much worse for her to deal with, though a year of living together might have muted the effects.

"The beast isn't going to attack any of us," said Tam. "It's looking for lone, vulnerable victims. That much we already know. It's also unlikely to be a match for all of us at once in an outright fight, and even one of us alone would give it a serious headache. We're not its ideal prey, after all."

Callum nodded. "Perry mentioned that beasts from the afterworld are hard to kill, but they can be banished with the right spell. That would work even if we stayed ignorant of what we're dealing with, wouldn't it?"

"Perry told you that, did she?" Maurice asked in unnecessarily belligerent tones.

"That's right." I spoke without looking at the vampire. "We might not know exactly what we're dealing with, but a general banishment charm would work. To do that, we'd ideally need to get it backed into a corner."

Tam inclined his head. "Exactly. That's the tricky part. We aren't searching for a spirit haunting a house, but something with a corporeal form that has an entire forest to hide in."

"And that only emerges when grabbing prey," added Maurice. "What, you think we should lay a trap with live bait?"

"One of us?" Callum wore a grimace of distaste. "Hell of a risk if it goes wrong."

"Not necessarily." Maurice's voice took on an anticipatory tone. "I bet it's itching to get into the tower. If all but one of us goes outside…"

"Maurice, we're not trapping that creature here in the tower," Tam said firmly. "The risks are too high."

"You just said we can't catch it outside." His shoulders slumped. "Why're you listening to her ideas and not mine?"

"Meaning me?" Once again, my mouth leapt in without consulting my brain. "Just because you woke up on the wrong side of the coffin—"

"You think you're so witty." He glared at the others. "What? It's true. She doesn't have the experience we do. You heard her the other day—she's never been part of a team before."

"You're the one being unnecessarily hostile." Farley rubbed her forehead. "I told you to cut it out. Go back to bed."

"You don't get to tell me what to do either." Maurice rose to his feet, his hands clenching. "Why'd you drag me down here if you're only going to ignore every suggestion I make?"

"Your idea poses too much of a risk to the rest of the team," Tam said. "We can certainly discuss ways of cornering the creature *outside* the tower, not inside, but until we agree on—"

Another boom of thunder interrupted, followed by a flash of lightning outside the window. Above our heads, the ceiling lights fizzled and died, plunging us into darkness.

"Oh, no," said Callum. "Not this again."

"The rain knocked out the power?" I shivered as a chill breeze swept through the room. The fire remained lit, but its reach only covered the area immediately in front of the flames, casting the rest of the room in shadow.

"That's why we have so many candles in here." Callum got to his feet and went to the bookcase, where I heard him opening a drawer underneath and rummaging around. "Might need a hand…"

Farley went to join him and immediately tripped over a chair in the darkness. "Who has the matches?"

"I do," Tam said. "The power will be back on within the hour, same as usual. It'll be fine."

I moved to help the others light small candles and put them on every surface in the room until we could walk around the chairs without tripping over. All of us except Maurice, who remained seated without volunteering to help. Vampires weren't fond of fire, I knew, but I wished he would go back to bed rather than infecting the rest of us with his bad attitude.

Back in my seat, another thought hit me. "Has the phone line gone down too? And the internet?"

"Most likely, yes," Tam said. "Like I said, it'll be back on soon, but I guess we'll have to wait a bit longer to hear back from Kellen."

"Bloody great," said Maurice.

"At least you have night vision." Farley tripped over a footstool on the way back to her seat and cursed. "I guess we're not cooking tonight?"

"Good luck calling for takeout without a phone signal," Maurice said.

Wonderful. It looked as though we'd be having cereal for dinner. "Says the guy who lives on dead rats."

The power did not return while the storm persisted, and the horror movie vibes didn't help the general mood inside the tower in the slightest. The others tried to start a game of cards, but with the need to use a candle to see by, the risks of starting a fire were too high. For once I understood Maurice's desire to sit as far from the rest of us as possible, considering how flammable vampires were.

Not that the roaring wind and crashing rain were particularly appealing either.

"Good job we went out when we did," I remarked to Tam. "If I were the monster, I wouldn't want to be out in that either."

Maurice flashed me a glare. "You went out, did you?"

"Perry and I took photos of the ritual scene," said Tam. "To send to Kellen so he can ask someone in the department to identify the symbols. They'll be visible to any wizard or witch who looks at the pictures."

"Too bad they can't text us the results," Callum said, checking his phone. "Still no signal."

"See, her ideas aren't all that great," said Maurice.

"It wasn't her idea, it was mine," Tam said. "What's the issue, Maurice? Perry isn't doing anything wrong."

He gave an incredulous laugh. "You can't see it? She's duping all of us."

What? Was he reading my mind again? I didn't think I'd had any thoughts that would justify this level of hostility ... unless he was jealous of me for going out alone with Tam. Maybe he thought I was trying to take his place in the team. That made sense, and the fact that I'd got him into trouble earlier probably hadn't helped either.

"Mind telling me how?" I queried. "Because it seems to me that you're the one being dishonest about the reason you're in such a foul mood."

Really, his reaction was way out of proportion. Was he

really that bothered about me going back into the woods with Tam? Part of me had wondered if he'd already known, given the presence Tam and I had picked up in the forest and hadn't been able to identify, but I hastily shut the thought down before the vampire picked up on the suspicions that had crossed my mind.

"Maurice," Tam said. "I don't want to have to discipline you, but if you think I'll give you the benefit of the doubt because you've been on the team for longer than she has, then you're mistaken."

If he'd spoken to *me* like that, I'd have considered taking him seriously, but Maurice merely scoffed. "Whatever."

He rose to his feet and left the room in the blink of an eye, while Farley released a breath. "Yikes. What's got him in such a mood?"

"I think," I said, "he's afraid he's being replaced. I'm not the mind-reader on the team, though, so I can't know for sure."

"Yeah..." Farley inclined her head. "Given what I'm picking up from him—a whole lot of resentment and jealousy—I'm gonna have to agree."

"He's jealous of you?" Callum blinked at me. "In that case, I'll go and talk some sense into him."

He climbed off his chair and followed the vampire out into the corridor, while the weight of Tam's gaze felt heavier than before. *Jealous.* Another new experience. The only thing I'd ever had that anyone might have envied was my closeness with Kellen, but to most people, he was just a supervisor, not the father figure he'd been to me.

This, though? This was new.

I turned to Farley instead. "Can your ability help to sense if someone's being untruthful or hiding something?"

"Good question." A thoughtful expression crossed her face. "It depends how good they are at keeping their emotions in check, but I can sometimes tell if someone's mood doesn't match the words they say aloud. Not quite as direct as mind-reading, but it can be an asset."

I'd guessed right, then, and she might have been able to gauge how much of Karl's confusion had been genuine when he'd come to the tower earlier. It was too late for that now, though, and I didn't think he was the one we needed to worry about.

Admittedly, Maurice's current behaviour almost made me less inclined to suspect him. Jealousy was such a human, petty thing, compared to the inhumanity that would make someone inclined to sacrifice a person to summon a heart-eating monster. Yet the question of who Tam and I had heard in the forest remained.

Tam moved in the direction of the cabinet. "I'm going to light more candles to put in the other rooms and near the stairs."

"I'll help," I offered, joining him at the cabinet and taking a box of matches from him.

Once we had the candles lit, we fumbled our way to the kitchen to make an entirely unsatisfying meal out of whatever scraps we could find that didn't need cooking. Maurice didn't reappear, though I supposed he could always snag a stray rat if he fancied a snack.

Upon returning to the living room, Farley tripped yet again and face-planted, luckily landing on the sofa. "You know, I sometimes wish I had night vision instead of being able to sense people's feelings."

"Do power cuts normally last this long?" I felt my way to another seat and sank into it.

"It varies." Farley rubbed her shin. "We need a game we can play in the dark."

"I'm going down to the training room to look for our spare chargers," Tam said. "Please try not to create any fire hazards while I'm gone."

"We have Cards Against Humanity," said Callum, when he'd left. "Might be a fire risk with those candles, though."

"Same with Monopoly," Farley commented. "How about hide-and-seek?"

"Sure, why not," I said. "As long as we avoid the candles."

After two rounds, both of which had resulted in one of us tripping over another, we ended up going to bed early to catch up on sleep instead of risking more injuries.

I dreamt of Maurice pursuing me through the woods again. This time he held a wand in his right hand and stood beside a summoning circle formed of shimmering symbols. Within lurked a dark shape, vaguely defined except for its sinister, glowing eyes…

The beast leapt, and I jolted upright, wide awake. My attention went to the window first, but a thump directly above my head made my gaze snap upward. Was someone in the attic? I hadn't looked in there since the first day, but the sound of the rain had finally quietened enough for me to hear other sounds. More thuds and soft thumps followed, also from above my head.

If Maurice had gone to take out his anger on the local rodent population, disturbing him wasn't the best idea, but I'd never settle back to sleep with disembodied noises above my head. It was highly unlikely the beast could have climbed all the way up the tower, especially as it would have been a lot faster and more convenient for it to have gotten in via the front door or one of the downstairs windows. But my paranoia was less convinced.

At another thud, I got out of bed, grabbed my wand, and slid my feet into slippers. After easing my bedroom door open, I conjured a small light that showed me that the door to the attic lay open a crack. *See? It's not the monster. It's one of us.*

Holding my breath, I approached the door and peered up the staircase, but the winding stairs twisted out of sight, preventing me from seeing into the room above. I took a hesitant step forward and then climbed slowly, trying to make as little noise as possible.

Inside the tiny room, Maurice sat cross-legged on the floorboards with a piece of chalk in his hand. There weren't any rats in here at all. What was he doing, then?

Eyeing me, he hissed out a breath of annoyance. "Go away."

"What are you doing up here?" I had to crouch to enter the tiny room, and it struck me that getting myself stuck in an enclosed space with a vampire was not my best idea. I knocked my head on the low ceiling and swore, the sound echoing, but he didn't move. Head throbbing, I took in the sight of him sitting in front of a mess of what appeared to be leaves. What had he been doing, raiding the ingredients supplies?

Wait. I knew that smell, not least because it was all over my clothes and the rest of the castle too. "What are you doing with that sage?"

"What do you think?" he challenged. "Get lost."

"Not if that's the sage we need to keep the monster

out." Whatever he was hiding might be none of my business, but now I looked closer at the floorboards, I detected several chalked symbols. Like… "You're dabbling in ritual magic."

Horror washed over me. It was *him*. I'd doubted my own suspicions and now he was using dark magic right above our own heads.

"Don't you start with the judgemental attitude," he said. "It's bad enough that you had to turn Tam against me."

"Does Tam know you're summoning beasts from the other side of the grave into the castle?" I stared at him, still unable to entirely believe it. "Why would you even do that?"

"You know why."

I really didn't. He'd also taken a major risk by sitting directly in front of the circle, though with his vampire's speed, he could probably get out of the way fast enough if the creature escaped.

Since when could vampires even use ritual magic, though? He'd been a wizard before being turned into a vampire, but he no longer carried a wand. Hence the chalk, I supposed, but my sense of disbelief and unreality persisted. "You must be out of your mind."

"You aren't seeing the bigger picture. Even Tam isn't."

"You've lost me." He really was out of his mind, and right now, he was more of a danger to me than the monster was. Yet he hadn't moved into a defensive position. Did he not believe I'd be able to take him on? "You were sneaking around the forest earlier, too, weren't you?"

"You really need to learn to mind your own business."

That was all the confirmation I needed to hear. I lifted my wand to cast a spell, but he dodged around me in a blur, moving down the stairs in the time it took to blink. I reeled back, almost falling after him. Catching my balance, I descended from the attic and sharply collided with someone else—Farley. She stumbled back a few steps with a yelp of alarm.

"Whoa," I said. "Sorry. Didn't know you were up. Where's Maurice?"

"He's pretty upset," she said. "What did you do to him?"

"Caught him trying to use ritual magic in the attic." I looked around for him, but the corridor was empty, and he might have run out of the tower for all I knew. "None of us is safe in here."

"Huh?" Her brow furrowed. "Have you been having nightmares? Sleepwalking?"

"No, I haven't been sleepwalking." How had he tricked even the empath on the team? "You can look up there for yourself if you want to see, but—where's Tam, anyway?"

"I think he went out."

"What do you mean, out?" Alarms blared in my skull. "At this time of night?"

"To check the defences around the tower, maybe. Don't ask me." She squinted at me. "Are you sure you weren't sleepwalking?"

"Maurice is running around the tower somewhere, and we have to find him." I ran to Tam's door and knocked, but the door nudged inward, revealing that the bed was unoccupied. He wasn't in. Farley was right. "Can you wake Callum and tell him Maurice has lost his mind?"

"Not you?" she said. "Because I'm picking up a lot of confusion from you at the moment."

"No. I'm a hundred percent serious. Maurice was drawing symbols in chalk on the floor up there, and he didn't even deny he was going to summon our monster. If he comes near you, run."

All my vampire hunting instincts were on full alert. Pity I didn't have a stake in an easily accessible location, but I could use an improvised weapon if need be.

I went down to the lower floor, using the light of my wand to illuminate the stairs so I didn't trip and break an ankle. A quick check confirmed Tam wasn't in the living room or kitchen either. That left the basement, and if he wasn't in there… no, Maurice hadn't hurt him to get him out of the way. Had he? *He wouldn't*. Or so I'd thought, but I couldn't be sure of anything anymore.

Heart in my throat, I took the stairs as swiftly as I dared. But before I could open the door to the basement, the front door rattled as if someone was shaking it from the outside.

Whoever it was, they were trying to get in.

13

My whole body tensed when the door rattled for the second time as if someone—or something—was doing their level best to shove it open by brute force alone. Raising my wand, I took a step back and collided with a solid form.

Twisting around, I breathed a sigh of relief when I recognised Callum's muscular frame in the darkness.

"What—?"

The door rattled again. Callum swore under his breath. "We've got company."

"You don't say." If I opened the door, we might end up nose to nose with the monster. With Maurice roaming around as well, it was risky … but if he'd been telling the truth, Tam was somewhere outside. "Tam's out there, I think. If that's the monster, we need to get it away from the door."

Another rattling sound shook the door. Raising my wand, I kicked it open and cast the brightest illumination charm I could muster.

In the blaze, someone cursed. *Tam.* Sure enough, our team leader stepped into view, squinting in the blazing light of my wand.

"Oops," I said. "I'm sorry. Did you get locked out?"

"Yeah … I left the key inside the tower by mistake." He shielded his face with both hands. "Sorry I scared you."

"It wasn't you." I glanced at Callum. "Not just you. We have a situation in here."

"Come again?" Callum peered upstairs. "Farley, is that you up there?"

"Is Perry still sleepwalking?" she called back.

"No, Tam got locked out of the tower, and we thought he was the monster." Callum turned to me. "Sleepwalking? Really?"

"I wasn't sleepwalking." I faced Tam. "I woke up when I heard some weird noises coming from the attic as if someone was crawling around up there. I went up to look, and I caught Maurice drawing chalk symbols on the floor. He was trying to summon … summon the monster."

Tam's brows shot up. "What? That can't be right."

"No way," said Callum. "He wouldn't do that."

"I bet he's the one who locked Tam outside too," I went on, breathing fast. "Seriously, he admitted straight up. Zero ambiguity."

"Oh, for crying out loud," said Maurice from the stairs. "I didn't know you were *that* paranoid."

I raised my wand and pointed it directly at him. "You know I'm not lying. The evidence is right there in the attic for anyone to see."

"I was trying to…" He trailed off when Tam entered the tower. "You can't take a hint, can you? Keep your nose out of my business."

"I have the right to know if my team members are taking risks inside our home," Tam said to him. "Maurice, I thought I told you *not* to entrap the creature within the tower."

"He…" I trailed off, recalling his earlier claim that it would be easier to banish the creature if we cornered it first. "You were trying to trap the creature in a circle of sage and then banish it?"

"Finally, the penny drops." He snorted. "This is our new team member, whose first instinct is to blame her teammates for committing the very crimes we're supposed to solve."

Heat flooded my face and neck. I'd thought he was confessing to being the original summoner, not trying to protect everyone—granted, by endangering lives in the process, but still.

"Anyone can make a mistake." I didn't know if I was talking to him, or to Tam, or everyone at once. "I wasn't the person doing dark magic in the attic of all places. And he also admitted he was sneaking around the forest earlier when we were at the crime scene too."

The vampire's pale face flushed. "You hardly have reason to criticise someone for taking action on their own, you know. I'd have thought someone with a curse on her would be a bit less judgemental."

His words hung in the air for a moment, as potent as a curse. *Curse. He knows.*

And now? Everyone else did too. Any response I might have conjured died in my throat. There was a long, painful silence before Tam said, "I'm disappointed in all of you."

"What did I do?" Callum sounded bewildered.

"You're supposed to keep the others in check when I'm not around."

"Don't shoot the messenger," Farley said. "Why *weren't* you around, anyway?"

"I was checking on our defences," Tam said. "I assumed you were responsible enough not to summon the creature we're hunting into the *attic*."

Maurice threw up his hands. "You're still blaming me even though she accused me of murder?"

"You're not exactly the picture of innocence, you know." As per usual, my mouth kept speaking without my permission. "Also, I didn't accuse you of murder. I accused you of summoning the monster. Which is true."

"Is nobody going to mention the elephant in the room?" Farley said. "What's this about a curse?"

My heart dropped, and then free-fell when Tam stepped in. "Right. Everyone in the living room. Now."

I couldn't say I hadn't seen this coming, but I'd thought I'd have more time to figure out how to explain, and I was far from mentally prepared to deal with the emotional fallout of my team learning my secrets.

He did this on purpose. Maurice might even have picked the information up on our first day and waited for the opportune moment to reveal it to everyone. Including Tam.

Frankly, I'd much sooner have gone outside to fight the monster single-handedly, but I had to see this through. In the living room, Tam halted in front of the main window, silhouetted by the moonlight streaming in from behind the low-burning candles, and surveyed our group.

"I don't need to reiterate the danger we're all in," he

said. "I should be able to leave the tower for a few minutes without one of you casting illegal spells and the rest of you getting into fights, shouldn't I?"

"The rest of us didn't do anything, technically," Farley said. "It was all those two. Maurice and Perry. Let them fight it out and see who wins."

"Honestly, I'm all in favour of that approach," I ventured. A fistfight could hardly make this situation worse, after all. "I can stake a vampire in my sleep."

"Dream on," growled Maurice. "Tam, what do you say?"

"I'd say you've earned yourself a disciplinary warning." Before I could feel more than a twinge of triumph, he looked sharply at me. "As for you, Perry, I'm going to give you the benefit of the doubt and assume you were concerned about the rest of us when you accused Maurice, but I thought you took being part of this team more seriously than that."

My face burned, and anger seared me at the gloating expression on Maurice's face. "I do take it seriously. I already admitted I made a mistake, which I would have realised sooner if Maurice hadn't run off instead of correcting me."

"I shouldn't have to justify myself to the likes of you."

Farley cleared her throat. "Can you please try to calm down until I'm out of the room?"

"Sorry." I might be able to block Maurice from reading my thoughts, but that didn't mean Farley wouldn't be able to sense our emotions.

"Right," said Tam. "Maurice, I want to talk to you alone. Perry, wait here. I'll talk to you afterwards."

He left the room, and the vampire followed a moment

later. Callum and Farley exchanged uncertain looks and then turned back to me. I wished they'd stop staring, but had I expected any less?

"What did Maurice mean by 'cursed'?" Farley finally asked. "You have a curse on you?"

"Supposedly." I lowered my gaze. "At any rate, every Seer I've met has told me that I have a bad-luck curse hanging over me. Nobody can agree on what that curse actually is, but it's pretty consistent."

"A bad-luck curse?" Farley asked. "How bad, exactly?"

"Bad enough that nobody at the Wardens' office wants to volunteer to accompany me on missions." No point in underplaying the issue. "That's why I was sceptical when Kellen assigned me to come here."

"No wonder you didn't want to be part of a team," said Farley.

"I didn't, not at first." I didn't miss the glance that passed between her and Callum as if they were assessing how quickly they could get away from me. "For the record, there's no way to tell if every minor inconvenience is due to the curse or not, but it wouldn't surprise me if that was the reason the power went out."

"That's not *too* bad," Callum said. "Also, it happens every few weeks anyway. Not usually in the middle of an important mission, mind you."

"That's the thing. We don't know." I drew in a breath. "It would have come out in the open whenever we next ran into a Seer, but I should have guessed Maurice would pluck the information from my head and use it against me."

"I don't know..." Farley trailed off. "Being cursed with bad luck is a pretty big deal when you're part of a team. We've had more than our fair share of bad luck already."

That was true enough. Painfully so. I didn't want to bring up my suspicions that Kellen had teamed us up precisely because of that commonality between us, but I'd already scuppered my chances of staying when I'd accused Maurice.

I could see where this was going. When it came down to it, they wouldn't want to take the risk of keeping me on the team. Maurice already wanted me gone. And Tam…

Well, if my luck held, he'd be next to show me the door.

Before either of them could say another word, I got up and left the room. Probably I ought to have left the tower, too, but I still had some self-preservation left, enough not to want to go out into the storm and either catch my death of cold or get killed by the monster. Instead, I went downstairs to wait outside the basement door for Tam to call me in for questioning. I might have tried eavesdropping on his chat with Maurice, but it wasn't as if it mattered at this point.

I already knew how it would play out. Tam would give him another chance despite him using deadly magic right on top of his teammates. He would have done the same for me, too, I had no doubt … but would he let a cursed witch stay in the tower?

The door opened, revealing a single large candle illuminating the basement. Maurice narrowed his eyes when he saw me outside, but he said nothing. Tam caught my eye over his shoulder and beckoned me into the room.

I entered, closing the door behind me. "Don't worry, I'll be out of here first thing in the morning."

Tam studied me, the darkness making it hard to see his expression. "Is that what you decided?"

"It's more what everyone else wants, not me. I've never had a say in this."

"I'm sorry you feel that way."

"It's not about me." I raised my gaze, forcing myself to look directly at him. "You heard Maurice. I'm cursed, and I don't want to force you to accept that risk. The others already voted me out."

"Hang on a moment." He blinked. "The others ... what? I already knew about the curse, if that's what the problem is. This isn't news to me."

"You know I'm cursed?" What—? "Kellen told you."

"Yes, he did," said Tam. "Like I said, I don't spread my team members' secrets around. I was waiting for you to feel secure enough to share with the others. I didn't count on Maurice being that hostile towards a newcomer."

"He's been going out of his way to get under my skin from the start." *He knew? Tam knew about the curse?* "You know he's never going to think of me as part of the team, and the others aren't going to side with the cursed newbie, are they?"

"It's not an either-or situation," Tam said. "For the record, I accepted Kellen's suggestion because I thought you'd be a good fit for the team, curse or no curse."

"You didn't tell the others, though." I shook my head. "Maurice got one thing right. I'm not a good fit here. I'm more comfortable staking a vampire than making friends with one, I made Farley pass out cold within a day, and Callum has chosen Maurice's side over mine already. What more proof do you need?"

"That isn't true," he said. "Farley can make up her own mind, and Callum likes you. So do I."

So do I. The riot of emotions his response stirred within me clashed with my self-defensive instinct, and as per usual, my mouth responded first. "Don't lie."

"I'm not lying," he said.

"You lied when you acted as if you didn't know that I'm a danger to everyone." Belatedly, dread hit me at the thought of him having known my deepest secrets from the moment he'd set eyes on me. "How much else did Kellen tell you?"

Everything. That, I was sure of. The illusion of being in control of my own story was just that. An illusion.

He'd known all along … and he'd still invited me to join the team. He'd even asked me to come with him into the forest, and he'd trusted me with his teammates' safety despite having every reason to do the opposite.

Tam took a step towards me, his mouth turning down at the corners. "I didn't want you to end up being this overwhelmed in the first couple of days here. I wanted you to settle into the team gradually, but this case is trickier than any we've dealt with in a long while. Emotions are high for all of us, which can cause people to say things in the heat of the moment that they regret later. Yes, including Maurice."

"Then what?" I asked. "Do you want me to wait for the others to cool down before they decide if they want to kick me out?"

"Nobody is getting kicked out." He glanced over at the desk and the papers strewn over it. "We're close to solving this case, I can tell. If not for you, Perry, we wouldn't have made it past the first step."

Heat flooded my face, this time not from humiliation at all. For once, I didn't even know what to say, but before I could formulate a reply, a sudden creaking noise echoed from outside the tower, followed by a low, inhuman growl that chilled me to the bone.

Silence spread between us, sharp as a knife. Tam went very still, then his hand moved towards the weapon at his belt.

"I think," I murmured, "it might actually be the monster this time."

Tam and I both advanced at the same time. He overtook me and opened the basement door, leaving one wooden barrier between us and the outside threat.

I raised my wand. "You want to open the door?"

"We need to see what we're up against." He moved closer to me, his breath feathering my neck and bringing goose bumps to the surface of my skin. "The sage will keep it from coming in. We're safe."

Another low growl from outside countered his words, but it didn't sound close enough for the beast to be close to the tower door. My heart thumped against my ribcage, louder. It might not be able to get in, but who knew what we were risking by opening the door?

"Right." This was ridiculous. I wasn't scared of the unknown, and to prove it, I reached for the door. "Ready?"

A shiver ran up my spine when Tam's hand brushed against mine from behind, and we pushed the door outwards to reveal our enemy.

My gaze travelled to the end of the gravel path next to the woods. All but indistinguishable from the surrounding forest, the beast resembled a deformed tree come to life, walking on its roots, branches splayed outward. I'd never seen anything like it before, but the creaking and swaying of its branches matched the noises we'd heard from the tower.

A low growl emanated from the creature when it saw the open door, and it lumbered forward on rooted feet. Gravel stirred as its heavy form picked its way forward, razor-sharp branches waving threateningly. Now I understood the gouge-like markings we'd seen near the site of the attack. Leaves scattered in its wake, but it came to an abrupt halt with a sudden chilling howl.

"There's a barrier of sage around the gravel path," Tam breathed. "It's clearly not a fan."

He was right. the creature wasn't moving any closer to the tower door, instead inching around the path while emitting odd growling noises. "Wait. Does that mean it's… undead?"

Was there such a thing as a zombie tree? If there was, I'd definitely never heard of one before. With a regular zombie, the one sure-fire way to be rid of it was by literally setting it on fire—a method that would be doubly effective on a tree—so I raised my wand.

Then I realised Tam was no longer at my side. He'd vanished from sight, and not back into the tower either. Instead, he walked out onto the gravel path, approaching the creature with his weapon in his hand.

"Tam," I whispered. "Don't."

I didn't dare cast a fire charm with him that close to our enemy, but Tam wasn't even looking at me, let alone listening. He continued down the gravel path, and the creature rotated with a loud creaking noise, watching him.

Wait. He was distracting its attention away from me. Seizing my chance, I raised my wand and sent a jet of flame towards the tree. A shriek escaped as a fiery blast of light engulfed the branches, erupting into billowing smoke and the smell of scorched leaves.

I took a step back, out of range, while the shrieking noise intensified. Amid the smoke, a shadowy blur detached itself from the tree, vanishing from sight into the forest.

As the smoke began to clear, Farley and Callum emerged from the tower. Maurice, too, though he retreated inside the instant he saw the smoke.

"What," Callum said, "is that thing supposed to be?"

"I believe it's a tree," I said. "Or it was before I killed it."

"You didn't kill it." Tam had returned to our side. "Did you see anything move away from the tree after you destroyed it? A ghostly figure, or something similar?"

"I saw a shadow … that was the creature?" Unfortunately, I had an inkling he was right.

"No doubt," said Tam. "A spirit of some kind. We destroyed its vessel, nothing more."

"There's a ghost that can possess *trees*?" said Maurice in incredulous tones.

Farley gave a wild-sounding laugh. "You can't be serious. Are you?"

"We all saw it with our own eyes," I said. "Didn't we?"

And if the beast was loose in the forest, then the threat wasn't over. Not by a long shot.

14

"I knew there was a reason I didn't trust nature."

Back in the living room, I sat down in an armchair, wishing I could have fallen into bed instead. The others' expectant stares were fixed on Tam and me, seeking an explanation as to how we'd ended up battling a tree. While I doubted any of them had forgotten our confrontation earlier, there was a more pressing issue at hand. Namely, our elusive monster. Maurice's clear bewilderment at the situation was the final nail in the coffin of my suspicion that he'd been involved in summoning the creature.

No traces were left of the tree itself since Tam had cleared them away, but the smell of smoke hung in the air and mingled with the low-burning candles around the room.

"Let me get this straight," said Callum. "We have a ghost that can possess trees? Did you kill it?"

"Not permanently," I said. "I have to say, it reminded

me of a freakier version of one of the Ents from *the Lord of the Rings.*"

Farley gave a choked laugh. "This is mad. If I didn't already say so."

"You did." Maurice seemed to have utterly forgotten his anger in the wake of the surprise tree attack. "Did any of you know it was possible for a ghost to possess a *tree?*"

His words addressed everyone, but the way he avoided looking in my direction made it clear he still viewed me as being on the outside of the team. Which was to be expected, really, but the reminder of our argument earlier called into question whether I'd stay to fight with them tomorrow.

I intended to, but only if the others all agreed to let me stay. And despite Tam's confidence in the team, I didn't know if they would.

"No," Callum replied to Maurice's question. "I didn't, but I can't see ghosts anyway."

That was to be expected. Even most witches and wizards couldn't see ghosts—or former witches and wizards, which would include Maurice as well as Farley and me—but this was no regular spirit.

"Regardless of which form they take, all spirits are essentially the same," Tam told us. "Yes, they're usually the Reapers' responsibility, but it'll take too long for the Wardens to contact them. Even if the power comes back on, we can't guarantee they'll arrive in time to prevent the beast from claiming another victim."

That figured. The Reapers were responsible for ferrying the dead to the afterworld, but when things unexpectedly escaped, the Reapers weren't always the first to know. Technically, the Wardens' job description covered *every* magical monster, including the ones that the Reapers were officially meant to handle. Besides, even if Kellen had direct contact with the Reapers, how many more people would die before they arrived?

"It might be dead, but it's still a monster." I spoke into the sceptical silence that followed Tam's words. "Which makes it our area of expertise."

"What's that mean?" Maurice stopped pretending to ignore me and gave me one of his customary scowls instead.

"I mean it's not unknown anymore," I clarified. "We know it's a spirit and that it's on the run without a host body. It's vulnerable."

"Exactly," Tam said. "As long as it isn't possessing a host, it can't kill anyone either."

"Just because it isn't ripping out hearts anymore doesn't make it less dangerous," said Farley. "Do you seriously want to go chasing after it? Now?"

"No, but I'm not giving up either," I said. "We have the advantage. Don't forget that."

"She's right," Tam said. "I'm still holding out hope that Kellen will reply to our messages and help identify the creature by the morning, but we know enough now to be able to figure out a plan of our own."

Nobody spoke, and my heart dropped a little. Sure, I knew why the others would be inclined to dismiss my ideas out of hand, but my curse had never interfered with my ability to hunt down dangerous monsters. If it had, I'd be out of a job.

I couldn't change their assumptions, though. Really, the signs that this wouldn't be an easy ride had been there from the moment Maurice had read my thoughts. Even

Stanley had recognised me as a danger to everyone around me without needing to peek into my mind.

Speaking of whom. With Maurice out, Stanley was officially back at the top of the suspect list, and once we'd got rid of the creature, our next priority should be to track down the person who'd summoned it to begin with. Nobody else had come up with any theories, and when the silence persisted among the group, I knew that I had to be the one to break it.

I also knew that Tam trusted me enough to want me to stay and that we'd had a real connection down there in the training room. Whether it would work out in the long term was another matter, but our battle with the creature had reminded me that I was far from the only team member with secrets.

Take Tam himself. He moved faster than any regular human should have the right to when he'd distracted the creature, and despite our earlier conversation about his commitment to keeping the team's secrets, I'd forgotten he had more than a few of his own.

I rose to my feet. "Agreed. For now, I think we should base our plan on Maurice's idea of luring the creature into a trap so we can cast a banishment spell. It's bound to be easier now that it no longer has a host body, isn't it?"

Maurice's jaw hung open for a moment. "Huh?"

His surprise was almost as satisfying as the evident approval in Tam's gaze when he inclined his head. I'd made the right call.

Farley shook her head firmly. "Oh, no. I don't want that thing in here."

"Not in the tower," I clarified. "Somewhere more sensible. Out on the path or even just inside the forest. If we put a circle of sage around the area that we entrap the creature in, it won't be able to get out. Might be the mistake the original summoner made."

Maurice's mouth closed. "It wasn't a mistake, I'm betting. They wanted the creature to get loose."

Yeah. I thought so.

"Most likely true," Tam added. "That said, it'll be hard to lure the creature into a trap, not when it already knows we're aware of its vulnerability."

"Unless we summon it." That, I was sure, was what Maurice had been planning to do in the attic. Summon the creature directly into a trap.

Maurice spun towards me. "*You* want to summon the creature, do you?"

"I didn't say that." I should have guessed that suggestion would touch a nerve, but short of letting the creature chase one of us through the forest, I couldn't think of a better way to get it into the trap.

"Our esteemed team leader already banned me from using ritual magic," said Maurice sourly. "Who gets to cast the spell, then?"

"Don't look at me," said Farley. "I wouldn't know where to start."

"And I can't use a wand," Callum put in.

As for Tam—well, I didn't know what kind of abilities he had, but he didn't carry a wand either.

Maurice's eyes narrowed—not at me, but at Tam. "I see how it is. You give me the lecture on responsibility and then let her do exactly the same as I did, is that it?"

"Maurice," said Tam in an exasperated tone, "I'm not letting anyone do anything. We're discussing strategies. I've already disciplined you for your earlier actions, and

I'm not going to repeat what I said about consulting the team *before* acting alone. That's the difference between then and now."

The vampire's shoulders slumped. "Right, fine."

"First things first," said Tam. "Clear the air, you two. I want you to apologise to one another and agree to start afresh, without any attempts to do anything that might sabotage our efforts to stop this monster."

Maurice's jaw tensed, and he didn't speak. One of us had to start, so I said, "I'm sorry I accused you of working with the enemy."

"I'm sorry I gave you that impression," he said, with apparent great effort. "And that I acted behind the backs of the rest of the team. Now can we move on? We need to trap that creature before it finds a new host."

"Ideally," Tam said. "With that said, it's close to dawn, so we have some leeway. The creature's likely to go into hiding until dusk, and it'll be weakened enough during the daytime that the banishment is also more likely to work."

"Unless it possesses one of us instead," added Callum.

"There is that risk," Tam confirmed.

"Not to me," said Maurice. "The dead can't be possessed. Including the undead."

Oh, of course. That explained why he hadn't brought anyone else into his misguided summoning attempt, but I'd already resolved not to start another argument with him, so I refrained from bringing that up.

Instead, I kept my tone carefully free from hostility when I addressed him. "That means you're less at risk if you help set the circle of sage to entrap the creature."

"And the rest of us are potential bait?" Farley snorted.

"Actually, that's not a bad idea. I'd like to see how that creature deals with possessing someone who already experiences everyone else's emotions on overdrive."

"It might not be able to possess humans at all," I said. "I mean, is a tree the most obvious choice of host?"

"No," Tam said in thoughtful tones. "It's not, which likely means there's a limit to the creature's capabilities. I'm going to try to get through to Kellen again and find out what he knows. One way or another, we should be able to put our plan into action by morning."

Our phone signal and internet connection were indeed back by the following morning, as I found out when my phone alarm woke me from sleep. I was surprised I'd managed to drift off at all, considering the upheaval of the night before, but exhaustion had won out in the end.

I got dressed quickly and prepared my weapons before going downstairs. Not even Maurice was in the living room, but the sound of thumping from the training room told me Tam was already up. Vampires were the only kind of paranormal I knew of who could move as fast as Tam had, but they definitely weren't early risers, which once again raised the question of what else he might be capable of. As I headed downstairs, I sternly told myself I was just going to ask him whether Kellen had replied instead of poking into his own collection of secrets. That would have to wait until after the creature was gone.

Assuming I was allowed to stay. The others hadn't brought up the curse again, and all our conversations the previous night had revolved around our plans for the morning. Like me, they had their attention focused on one task: getting rid of that monster and arresting the person responsible for summoning it.

It wouldn't last forever, but for now, I pushed open the door to the training room, finding Tam in the same spot as the previous day. His fists pounded the punching bag, and heat rose to my face at the memory of our closeness the previous day.

"Perry," he said, without turning around.

"Hey," I said. "Signal's back."

"I know," said Tam. "Kellen got back to me and said the ritual was definitely used to summon some kind of demonic spirit. I had to narrow it down from there."

"Did you tell him it possessed a tree?"

"I did. Check out the notes on my desk."

I walked over to the desk, where Tam's notebook was opened to a fresh page with notes scrawled onto it. "A Class One demonic spirit? That's what we're dealing with?"

"Kellen sent me his research." Another thump of the punching bag. "Class One spirits can latch on to living creatures, but they have trouble with humans and even animals. They're confined to weaker forms, though they're able to warp and animate them to their will."

"Lovely." Good to have confirmation that it wouldn't be able to possess any of us, though. "At least nobody will need to volunteer as bait."

The spirit was dangerous to humans even in its current state, especially as it needed to devour human hearts to maintain its grip on its host body. And in a forest, there was no shortage of potential options.

"There is that," Tam said. "I think we'll have to persist

with our plan to summon and then banish the beast, and Kellen gave me the go-ahead to use any means necessary to get rid of it. That okay?"

"Of course." At least I didn't need to worry about being possessed on top of all the other ways that creature could maim us. "A summoning spell isn't that hard to cast."

"That's not why I asked. I meant are you still okay with … all of this."

I frowned, unsure what he was getting at. Then it clicked. He still thought I planned to leave after the mission was done.

"I'm still in," I told him. "I'll deal with this monster, find the culprit, and … I need to talk to Kellen and ask a few questions, but that can wait until later."

"Questions about how much he told me?" he guessed. "Your secrets are safe with me, Perry, don't worry."

Even from Maurice? "I'm not going to start another feud, but … well, we do have a mind-reader in the tower."

"I've trained to keep my thoughts from being read," he said. "Even if Maurice breached our agreement and read my thoughts, he wouldn't find anything on you, don't worry."

He'd trained to keep his thoughts from being read? That wasn't an easy skill to master at all. Once again, curiosity reared its head, but I couldn't trust myself to ask any questions without screwing up again. Besides, I'd be a hypocrite to judge him for wanting to keep his own secrets under lock and key.

"All right." I raised my head at the sound of footsteps upstairs. "I think the others are awake."

"Then we'd better join them," said Tam.

On the way upstairs, his phone started to buzz with an

incoming call. He halted outside the kitchen to answer, while I went inside and found Callum trying to make coffee with cold water instead of boiling the kettle. Needless to say, he wasn't having much success.

"I'll make it," I offered. "Your eyes aren't even open yet."

He brightened considerably. "Thanks."

"Can I have one too?" Farley asked from the doorway.

"Sure." Maybe that was the key to friendship—offering to make everyone coffee. Except for one person, of course. "I don't know if Maurice drinks coffee, but I draw the line at mixing his with blood."

Maurice himself cleared his throat from where he'd appeared against a wall, unseen. "No, thanks. Caffeine has no effect on me."

"The horror." Callum shuddered and took the mug I offered him. "Thanks."

As I distributed the mugs around the table, Maurice looked on from his standing position, somehow projecting an impression of impatient restlessness despite his complete stillness.

"So," he said when everyone was seated, "when are we going to trap and kill this beast?"

"Calm down," I told him. "Tam has some new notes on the creature that Kellen sent over when he was able to reply to his message. Our beast is a Class One demonic spirit. It can't possess humans, though it seems to rely upon consuming human hearts to maintain its form."

Maurice blinked. Once. "What does that mean for our plan?"

"For a start, nobody needs to act as bait."

"Well, that's a relief." Farley's shoulders notably

relaxed, though she retained a wary air. "We can still banish it, though, right?"

"We can," I confirmed. "Our plan should work as planned."

"Not quite." Tam stood in the doorway, his expression considerably less optimistic than in our last interaction. "Janessa just called. Apparently, Reynard has gone missing."

"Missing?" I echoed. "What do you mean by that?"

Did the creature possess another tree and ambush him?

If so, why pick Reynard of all people as its victim? Had he been wandering in the woods even after our warnings?

"He vanished from his house this morning," said Tam. "The police found signs of a struggle, so they suspect foul play."

"But…" That made no sense. "Since when did the creature leave the forest and visit people's houses in search of prey?"

"We must have driven it to desperation," said Maurice. "We should have summoned it right after it left its former host body behind. Now someone else is dead."

"He might still be alive," said Tam. "According to Kellen, it takes a while for the creature to gather the strength to possess another host body after one is destroyed, so I have my doubts that it found one that soon. In fact, I'm not convinced Reynard was taken by the creature at all."

"What, did someone else kidnap him?" This was a development I hadn't seen coming and not one that I would have connected to the case if not for the fact that the victim was one of our suspects. "Weird."

"I think we should talk to Janessa in person and check

Reynard's house for clues about who might have taken him," said Tam. "If the creature isn't responsible, then the police will have to take over."

"Yeah, it shouldn't be our problem if someone else has decided to start kidnapping random locals," said Maurice. "Don't look at me like that, it's true."

I hadn't *liked* Reynard, finding his attitude towards the victims callous at best, but that didn't alter my concern at the creature's apparent change in behaviour. As for Maurice... "That's right. If we confirm the monster didn't take him, we can go straight to the forest to put our plan into motion."

He looked momentarily surprised at my agreeing with him, as did the others—except Tam. He knew, as did I, that if it took forming an alliance with a vampire to reach our goals, then I'd do whatever was necessary.

One way or another, we'd wrap up the case by the day's end. I'd make sure of it.

15

Leaving the tower behind, our group set off for Hexworth. I might have suggested taking one of the hiking trails through the woods to save on time, but we'd run the risk of encountering the monster again before we were ready. Tam had decided that we'd be better off talking to the police first and finding out about this newest disappearance before we decided whether to go ahead with our plan regardless of Reynard's strange absence.

"I'd have thought Stanley would be the first to vanish, if anything," I remarked as we walked down the road through the centre of the village. "Given that he spends all his free time wandering around the forest."

Stanley would likely stand a better chance at fending off potential attackers than Reynard was, but unless Reynard had been near the forest himself, it made no sense for him to have been targeted.

"Yeah, tell me about it," Farley said. "Maybe a disgruntled customer decided to take revenge."

"They picked a hell of a time to strike, when everyone's already on edge," said Callum. "No, I don't think this is unconnected with the monster."

"Agreed." Tam halted outside the police station. "I'll go in alone. You wait out here."

While he went to talk to the police, the rest of us listened through the partly open door.

"When did anyone last see Reynard?" Tam asked Janessa.

"Yesterday evening," she replied. "All the signs show that he was dragged out of his home late last night. Some of his neighbours heard a disturbance, but they followed our instructions to stay indoors after dark and didn't see who took him."

"So, you don't know for sure that there's a connection with the beast in the forest," Tam concluded.

"No, but I find it difficult to believe the timing is coincidental," she said. "Has your team made any progress on the case?"

"We encountered the creature again last night and were able to identify it as a low-powered demonic spirit," said Tam. "It's unable to move around without a host body, and we destroyed its last one, leaving it weakened and vulnerable."

"What do you mean by 'destroyed'?" she asked. "By host body, you can't mean a human?"

"No … a tree." I had to admire Tam for keeping his tone as serious as he did, given the absurdity of his words. "The beast isn't strong enough to take on a human host, so it went for the nearest target."

Janessa made a disbelieving noise. "A *tree*? I do hope you're not lying to me."

"Not at all," Tam said. "It's our intention to get rid of the beast before it takes on another host body. However, its choice of host makes me question if Reynard's unfortunate disappearance was the creature's responsibility. He doesn't live close to the woods, and I find it hard to believe that a host body of that size would have been able to break into his home. Did you find any signs—leaves, soil—that suggested that might be the case?"

"No." Janessa's tone suggested part of her still believed Tam was having her on. "All the signs pointed to a human being responsible for the break-in, but a human summoned the beast to begin with, did they not?"

"True," Tam said. "Then it's possible that the summoner was responsible for taking Reynard, though I can only speculate on why that would be."

"Then by all means search the house itself for clues," said Janessa. "Whatever the case, I sincerely hope nobody else needs to die before this rogue monster is put down."

"As do I." Tam exited the police station, surveying our group. "Is everyone fine with the idea of searching Reynard's house before going into the forest?"

Murmurs of agreement followed, though like me, they evidently had doubts that the creature could have possibly got into someone's house and kidnapped someone when it was supposed to be either a disembodied ghost or in the form of a tree. The townspeople might not have witnessed the first victim being dragged into the forest, but one would think a tree walking through the middle of the village would have drawn attention.

"This can't be our monster's work," I said to Tam as we walked away from the police station. "If it possessed another tree, its roots would have dug up the road, and there'd be mud and leaves everywhere."

"You aren't wrong, but it's possible the creature picked a different host body this time," said Tam. "Not a human one… that ought to be beyond its strength, according to the notes Kellen sent me."

"Might he have been mistaken?" Farley asked in a tremulous voice. "Underestimated its strength?"

"No." Callum moved to comfort her. "I'd say Reynard made himself another enemy or two."

Nothing would surprise me at this point, but I certainly didn't see any signs of tree-related carnage as we walked to Reynard's house, which looked the same as usual except that the door was slightly ajar.

"The police said the door had been forced or opened by magic," Tam said. "Definitely a human's doing."

I followed Tam into the house and immediately spotted an open trapdoor leading down into a cellar or basement. "Reynard said he slept in the basement when we spoke to him, didn't he? How would the beast have known that?"

"It wouldn't." Tam led the way to the trapdoor, where a ladder descended into a small cave-like room. A camp bed lay on its side in the corner with its covers strewn across the floor as if a struggle had taken place. There wasn't any blood, nor any obvious signs of an injury—and no twigs or leaves from outside either.

"Looks like it really was a regular old kidnapper." Farley's voice shook with relief. "Did Reynard figure out who the summoner was, do you think? Is that why someone took him?"

"I have my doubts." I thought back. "Perhaps one of

Reynard's former customers decided to leave him as bait for the monster as payback for selling a dodgy potion."

That was a stretch, I'd freely admit, but I was low on ideas. I circled the trapdoor and tripped over a pair of shoes that had clearly been worn outside recently; they were caked in mud and leaves.

"He left his shoes behind too." I picked them up and placed them against the wall so nobody else fell over them, and my gaze caught on a trail of leaves and herbs sprinkled along the wall. They smelled familiar. *Sage.*

I backed down the hallway, following the line with my gaze. Someone had carefully trailed sage across the edge of the wall, and I was willing to bet they'd done the same in the house's other rooms too. "Hey, look at this."

"Sage." Callum followed my line of sight. "How would he know to put it around his house?"

"It's common enough knowledge that it repels the dead," Tam said. "Whatever the case, I doubt we'll find any more clues in here. The police have already searched the entire house."

All the same, unease stirred within me. Reynard might have taken steps to protect his house, but he was defenceless outside. Was that why the attacker had dragged him out of his place of safety? *Why him, though?*

"It's not our problem," said Maurice. "Like you said— it's the police's responsibility to deal with his disappearance. The monster hasn't been here since yesterday."

"I don't know…" I paused. "I think we should look around the edges of the forest, near the site of the attack yesterday, in case there's a clue pointing to Reynard's location."

"Good idea," Tam said. "We can see if Reynard left any other clues behind on the way."

Leaving the house behind us, we made our way to the stone wall bordering the forest. Tam's pace quickened when we caught sight of Karl standing near the wall, wearing his cardboard armour and an agitated expression.

Karl came hurrying over the moment he saw us. "I'm so glad you came!"

"Why's that?" Tam asked. "What's going on?"

"I heard screaming from old Stanley's house!" he exclaimed. "I tried knocking on the door, but he wouldn't answer."

"Stanley?" I echoed. "Was he the one screaming?"

"I don't think so." His voice hushed. "Reynard is missing. Is that true?"

Stanley. I glanced over at Tam, whose expression had turned grim. *Stanley* had taken Reynard captive. Why, I could only guess, but I should have expected something like this. If Stanley was indeed the person who'd summoned the beast, then he'd be furious at us for removing the demonic spirit from its host. Angry enough to strike back—but why target Reynard instead of one of us? Did he think we were friends?

"Thanks for telling us," Tam said. "You should go to the police. They'll want to know too."

"We'll let you know how it turns out," I told him. "After you tell the police, you're better off lying low until we've dealt with the problem."

"Well, then, I wish you all the best of luck."

He bounded away, awkward in his cardboard armour, while the rest of us faced the swathe of trees before us. I didn't see any obvious traces, but if I had to guess, Stanley had dragged Reynard directly through the bushes to his cottage. While I'd distrusted the guy from the start, though, a nagging voice in the back of my mind told me that his decision to target Reynard made little sense.

Tam faced our group one last time. "I don't know what's going on in there, but we need to be prepared to deal with anything. Stay close together, and nobody wander off unless I give the order. That clear?"

A collective murmur of assent came from the others. Even Maurice didn't raise an objection, for a wonder, and this time we made no effort to hide ourselves as we took a direct route through the woods towards Stanley's cottage.

Tam halted before we came within reach of the door. "Keep both eyes open for traps," he murmured. "Remember—there are defences all over the cottage."

"It's lucky Karl didn't run into any." I frowned. "Didn't he say he knocked on the door?"

"He knows Stanley," said Tam. "If I had to guess, the security spells are rigged to target any intruders but to leave his friends alone."

"Friends." I made a sceptical noise. "The guy's a menace. Does he even know Reynard?"

"Let's find out." His expression turned serious, all business. "Maurice, can you scout around and tell me if there are any traps in the trees?"

The vampire disappeared in a blur and then returned in the time it took to blink. "None. They're all on his house, I assume."

"That makes it easier," said Tam. "Perry, you and I will lead the way to the house. When we're within sight, cast a revealing spell."

"Are you sure?" I asked. "That'll definitely tip him off."

"That's the intention," he said. "The time for subtlety is over."

Now we were talking. "Good."

"Maurice, take Farley and Callum around the back," Tam said in a low voice. "You need to be ready to ambush him if he makes a run for it, which I suspect he will."

"Got it."

I raised my wand, and Tam and I approached Stanley's ramshackle hut. I didn't hear any screaming or other sounds pointing to Reynard's presence, but Stanley might have used a silencing spell or worse to ensure his prisoner didn't give himself away again.

With a wave of my wand, a swathe of vibrant symbols appeared in the air, spreading all over the hut's exterior like a rippling carpet. No wonder the monster hadn't been able to get in, what with the layers of spells designed to trip, paralyse, and otherwise incapacitate any threat that went within a metre of the door. There must also be a spell in there to pick up on whether someone was hostile or not, given their lack of effect on Karl.

Tam and I, on the other hand, wouldn't be that lucky.

"I have to undo all those spells for us to approach the door." I readied myself, flexing my wrist. "He'll know the instant I do, though."

"I'm ready." He didn't budge, but he kept a hand on his weapon as I raised my wand.

With a rush of determination, I cast a negation spell and directed it at the entire hut. The security spells unravelled like a thread unspooling, but Stanley didn't appear. Nor did Reynard make a sound. Weird, though my theory of Stanley having used a silencing spell on him might yet prove to be accurate.

With the defensive spells undone, our path to the hut was clear. I nodded to Tam, and we drew closer until I could peer through the window. A figure sat in the corner of the room, wrists and ankles bound. *Reynard.* I didn't see Stanley, however, and silence filled the surrounding forest. My skin crawled. What was he playing at? I hadn't a clue, but someone had to get Reynard out of there.

"I'll grab him," Tam murmured. "Are all the spells on the house taken care of?"

"Yes, but there might be more on the inside that I couldn't detect." I trod closer. "If the window can open wide enough for him to climb out, we won't have to go through the door. Let's see."

I flicked my wand again. My unlocking charm caused the window to spring open, and Reynard raised his head in surprise. As his startled gaze met mine, I pointed my wand through the open window and cast a spell to undo the bonds around his feet and hands. He didn't make a sound, but I'd lift whatever spell had silenced him when he was safely outside.

"Come on," I hissed. "Get closer to the window so we can help you climb out."

Reynard didn't need any further encouragement. He inched closer to the window, where Tam waited to help him climb up onto the sill.

Then the sound of snapping twigs made me spin on my heel.

"I thought I heard someone sniffing around here." Stanley stepped into view from behind a tree. "Messing with my security spells too. I should have you arrested."

I raised a brow at him. "And kidnapping an innocent person isn't worthy of arrest?"

"He's not innocent," he said. "You're in more danger than you know, especially if you continue to remove the spells keeping that creature away from here. I'm not the one you should be worried about. *He* is."

He pointed at Reynard, who flinched but continued to clamber out the window until he touched down beside Tam.

"Did he use a silencing spell on you?" I raised my wand and cast a reversal charm, and he let out a breath of relief. To Stanley, I added, "Karl heard the screaming, so I figured you'd have made sure nobody else did."

"That busybody couldn't leave well enough alone," Stanley growled. "He doesn't have a clue what this man is capable of, and neither do you."

"Can't be worse than the beast haunting the woods," I said. "We came here to get rid of it and to hand the person responsible for summoning it over to the police. Our entire team has you surrounded, so if I were you, I'd come quietly."

"You're accusing the wrong person," Stanley said softly. "Fools."

A thud drew our attention to Reynard. Out of nowhere, he'd made a sudden break for it—but he'd slammed straight into Maurice. The vampire held his arm in a grip that looked casual from the outside, but I knew from painful experience how impossible it was to free oneself from a vampire's hold without breaking a bone in the process.

Keeping a firm grip on Reynard, Maurice looked

directly at Tam. "I looked into his mind. He's the one who summoned the beast. Reynard is."

Oh. Oh, no. There was no hiding the truth from the vampire, and when Reynard's gaze lowered, I knew Maurice wasn't lying.

"See what I mean?" Stanley said. "Now you've endangered us all."

"You tied a man up inside your own house instead of going to the police?" It was entirely typical of Stanley, but that didn't make me any less exasperated with him. "What did you plan to do to him, exactly? Force a confession with nobody but you to hear it?"

"I planned to make him get rid of that *thing* he summoned before it killed anyone else," he retaliated. "But you had to barge in and ruin everything by setting him loose."

"We came here to get rid of the creature ourselves," Tam told him. "Maurice, keep hold of Reynard. I'll fetch the others."

"You don't know what you're doing," Reynard croaked, looking pale. "You can't beat that monster."

"Hardly." Tam's voice was cold. "Come on. We'll find somewhere less exposed."

"Preferably somewhere away from my house, if you don't mind," Stanley said to our retreating backs.

Reynard struggled against Maurice's grip, to no avail. "Help! Let me go!"

Nobody listened to a word he said, though I was tempted to cast another silencing spell to stop him from drawing attention as we walked deeper into the woods until Stanley's cottage was out of sight. Farley and Callum joined us—both wearing stunned expressions at the sight of Reynard held in Maurice's grip—but they swiftly moved to obey Tam's commands when they grasped the situation.

Following the original plan, we placed a circle of sage around a contained area, with all of us standing outside of it. Then Maurice handed Reynard over to Tam.

"Stop!" Reynard shrieked, as Maurice took a piece of chalk in hand and began to draw out a summoning circle on top of the blanket of leaves littering the ground. "That beast is too dangerous to be contained!"

"You summoned it!" I pointed out. "You sacrificed your friend in the process, too, didn't you? Don't lie."

He began to sob. "I didn't. We … we did the spell together."

"For what purpose?" Tam enquired. "What were you trying to summon, exactly?"

"I heard…" He gasped and gulped, tears streaming down his face. "I heard there's a booming market for certain types of spirit that can be trapped inside objects and sold."

"You wanted to trap the spirit in a jar and sell it?" I asked incredulously.

"It was all my idea." He kept sobbing. "He … he offered to help me. We thought two would be enough people to react if anything went wrong, but when that creature appeared—it lunged straight out of our circle and killed him. It'll do the same to you too."

"You're a fool," said Tam. "Perry, are you ready?"

For what? Oh, right. He expected me to be the person to cast a summoning spell to bring the spirit into our trap, and his show of faith in me brought an unexpected spike of nerves.

I waved my wand in a figure-eight pattern and murmured under my breath. The actual words of the spell didn't matter, really, but they kept me focused as I repeated the wand movements until a gust of wind swept across the circle, rustling the leaves and raising the hairs on my head.

Then a patch of darkness appeared above the symbols, resembling more of a cloud than a living being. Maurice bared his fangs, while Farley hissed out a breath. *That's our spirit.*

Tam reached for his weapon, and Reynard twisted free of his grip and bolted across the clearing. As he did so, the shadowy being swarmed across the ground and after him.

"Scumbag." Maurice took an alarmed step back. "He smudged the circle."

In his wild flight, Reynard had kicked a gap in the circle large enough for the shadowy beast to ooze out, the darkness swarming over the leafy ground and up the trunk of a nearby tree.

A creaking, groaning noise escaped the tree, and on instinct, I waved my wand and sent a jet of fire at it. The tree ignited in flames, but the smoke billowing outwards had the unfortunate side effect of masking the beast from sight. I couldn't see if it was still inside the tree or not.

"Don't burn down the forest with us inside it," Maurice hissed.

I flicked my wand, conjuring a faint breeze in an attempt to drive the smoke away from our faces. "Got a better idea for taking down a possessed tree?"

"Hey!" Tam's voice rang out. Somehow, he'd moved to the other side of the clearing, having caught Reynard in his grip once again. "This is the one you want. Isn't it?"

As the smoke dispersed a little, I spotted the shadowy outline of the creature stirring amid the smoking ruins of the tree. As it began to ooze towards Tam, I pointed my wand directly at it and cast a banishment spell.

"No good," Stanley growled from behind my shoulder. "It's still holding on to its vessel."

"Then what?"

A deafening bang shook the clearing as Stanley fired his gun at the tree. A horrific screech ripped across the clearing, and the patch of darkness flew out into the open.

My ears ringing, I cast the banishment spell again. A blast of light struck the darkness, which blurred before our eyes and then vanished into the light.

It's over.

16

To no surprise, the instant the creature vanished, Reynard tried to make another break for it. Luckily, I wasn't the only one who'd seen it coming. Maurice caught him by the arm, while Stanley pointed his gun directly at his face. Reynard's shoulders slumped, all the remaining fight going out of him, and that was that.

"That's better," Tam said. "You're going to stay put while we clean up this mess. That clear?"

Reynard nodded meekly. As the person who'd caused most of the destruction, I figured it was my job to clean up—specifically, putting out the fires I'd started amid the trees in my efforts to corner the creature. As per usual, I was better at creating messes than cleaning them up, and as I extinguished the last pile of smoking leaves, I caught sight of Stanley glowering at me.

"Sorry I accused you of summoning that monster," I said awkwardly. "And for taking down the security spells on your house."

He grunted. "At least you were courteous enough to move away from my house before setting things on fire."

Coming from him, that was almost a friendly overture. It helped that Reynard was the primary target of his animosity, and with the monster taken care of, I could get on with doing my level best to stay out of his way.

And stay out of the forest, but that was a given.

With the clearing returned to its former state and no traces of the battle remaining in the forest, we hauled Reynard to the police station. Tam did most of the talking, and Janessa had let him speak without asking questions for the most part. Even after Reynard had been carted off to the little jail adjacent to the police station, there wasn't much space for us to manoeuvre with all of us crammed into the main room. Maurice and Farley were not thrilled at being trapped in a small room with so many people, but Janessa had made it quite clear she wanted all of us present while we explained what had taken place.

"So, it's gone," Janessa said when Tam had finished describing our clash with the beast. "The creature."

"Back to the afterworld where it belongs," I confirmed. "It won't be escaping again in a hurry."

"Not on my watch," added Stanley, who'd refused to leave the police station until he was sure Reynard had been incarcerated. "I'll make sure of it."

Strangely enough, I believed him. He might be a grumpy and paranoid old man who hated outsiders, but he'd seen through Reynard's pretended innocence before anyone else had. Granted, we might have figured out the culprit sooner if we'd set our resident mind-reader on him … not that I wanted to remind Maurice of that fact.

He'd come through for us in the end, but that didn't mean I needed to give him another excuse to act as if he was superior to the rest of us. He'd been smirking nonstop since we'd hauled Reynard out of the forest.

With Reynard taken care of, it was time to go back to the tower. When we left the police station, we found the streets almost deserted. I suspected it'd be a while before the people of Hexworth stopped avoiding the hiking trails. Or at least carrying sage in their pockets.

We did run into Karl on the road out of town, and I reassured him that he could go back to using the forest to practise his roleplaying again.

"Ah, good," he said. "Thank you for your service. You're all true heroes."

"We're not…" Callum trailed off when he departed, still clad in his cardboard armour. "Heroes."

"I think we should enjoy our success." Maurice sauntered ahead. "Bask in the glory for a while."

"I agree," Tam said. "That wasn't how I expected things to play out, but I'm impressed at how you handled the situation when Reynard was revealed as the killer. That was some quick thinking back there—especially on your part, Maurice. And you, Perry."

He pointed at Maurice and then at me. The vampire's smirk widened, but I felt myself flushing. Let's face it, I didn't think I'd done anything too admirable back there. I'd picked out the wrong culprit for the second time in as many days, and it'd taken Maurice's mind-reading power to get to the truth. Not that I needed to stroke his ego at the expense of my own.

"Thanks," I settled for saying. "I was improvising, mostly. I didn't expect the monster to escape the circle."

"That wasn't Reynard's most sensible decision," said Tam.

"Has he made any at all?" Maurice said. "I don't buy into his claims that he summoned that thing by accident either. He didn't expect that particular spirit to show up, sure, but that doesn't mean he wouldn't have tried to trap it in a bottle and sell it online if he could get away with it."

"He also let his friend take the fall," I added. "I wonder if those dodgy potions of his have hurt anyone too."

"Exactly," said Tam. "My guess is that Stanley always had an eye on him for that reason."

"Pity he didn't go to the police before kidnapping the guy," added Farley. "He seems to distrust authority figures, but that's no excuse to act like a vigilante. What if Reynard had escaped his house?"

"Yes, I intend to have a firm chat with him later," Tam said. "It'd help to have him willing to trust the Wardens with any future concerns, though, so I won't be too harsh on him."

I doubt he will. Not as long as I'm around, anyway. Though, I didn't have to worry about running into him again as I intended to avoid the forest.

"What now?" asked Farley. "Can I break out the wine now?"

"Not quite," Tam said. "We still need to send a report to the office detailing how we caught and banished the demonic spirit. Preferably by tomorrow morning."

Everyone groaned. I'd known we'd need to send a report to Kellen, who was no doubt waiting with bated breath for news, but I still owed him a phone call too. Now the case was done, I had no excuse to put it off any longer.

Once we arrived back at the tower, we got to work right away. With the whole team involved, it wouldn't be as hard to pull together a report of the past few days, despite the challenge of making our many misadventures sound vaguely professional. Tam did the actual writing, typing straight onto his laptop, while the rest of us chimed in with reminders.

"We're not going to include all our wrong turns, are we?" Maurice eyed me. "Because if we have to list all the times the wrong person ended up being accused, then it's only fair to mention that that was mostly due to one team member, not the rest of us."

Tension rippled through the room. *He just had to ruin the mood.* Admittedly, it wouldn't be the first time that issue had shown up in one of my mission reports, but there'd never been other people liable to take the fall as well as me.

"Maurice," said Callum sternly. "We only solved the case because Perry was willing to keep pushing, to keep investigating, until we came to the right answer. If we'd stayed put in the tower instead of confronting the creature head-on, forcing it to reveal its form and destroying its host, where would we be?"

"Exactly," Farley said. "Do you want to drop in a mention of how one team member tried to mess with necromancy in the attic as well?"

"No." Maurice slumped in his seat. "Stop ganging up on me."

"We'll stop reminding you of your mistakes if you return the favour," I added. "Ah … Tam, you *aren't* putting any of that in the report, are you?"

"Of course not," Tam answered. "It was a challenging case. We did the best we could with the knowledge we had available, and I've made that clear in the report. They only need the basics—the creature's appearance and attacks, our plan to corner it, Reynard's disappearance, and our subsequent investigation leading us to the culprit…"

"And how we kicked the monster back into the after-world," Farley finished. "Good enough for me. Can I get out the wine now?"

"If you like," said Tam, reading over the report on his laptop screen. "I'll email this to Kellen's office. I've already messaged him telling him that we triumphed over the beast and handed the culprit over to the police."

"Good." My own phone lay untouched on the arm of my chair, a reminder of the decision I needed to make. Soon.

Tam typed on the keyboard. "I'll also request that our next mission should be somewhere that isn't quite as close to the tower."

"Our next mission," I repeated. "Is that how it usually works? Straight from one mission to the next?"

"We have a reprieve for a few days." He looked up from his laptop screen. "That is if you're still certain you're staying."

Nobody said anything. Maurice's expression was blank, but Callum looked hopeful, and Farley gave me an encouraging smile.

I drew in a breath. "Yeah … if the curse isn't a deal-breaker for anyone. I've told you everything I know, which I realise isn't much, and isn't a guarantee of anyone's safety."

"Pretty sure that's our entire job description," Callum remarked. "Right, Farley?"

"True," she said. "Though … is it possible for you to find who cursed you and get them to remove it?"

"If I knew who it was, I'd have already asked them," I replied.

"You don't know who cursed you?" Maurice sounded more curious than mocking. "How did you walk into a curse without knowing?"

"It happened when I was an infant," I told him. "So no, I don't know who cursed me. Since most curses can only be removed by the caster, nobody else has been able to shift it. Kellen's entire department has tried, in fact. They concluded that there's nothing to be done."

"Harsh," said Farley. "For the record, I don't find it a deal-breaker. It's hardly worse than being able to feel everyone else's emotions at all times."

"Same," Callum said. "I admit it freaked me out a bit at first, but that's because we've dealt with a few dodgy curses in our time. If someone cursed you as an infant and you're still walking, we're probably safe."

"The effects can hit other people," Maurice said. "Right?"

"Technically, yes, but it's difficult to prove when it does," I said. "Only Seers seem to be able to detect that there's a curse on me at all. Also, Kellen has spent more time around me than anyone else and he's still breathing, so there's that."

"Exactly," Tam said. "I think we can all agree that we've dealt with worse than curses in the past year, can't we?"

Maurice gave a slow, begrudging nod. "Sure, but if lightning strikes the tower, we know whose fault it is."

"Maurice!" Farley exclaimed. "Can you not be a nuisance for five minutes?"

"No."

I let them argue, a smile tugging at my mouth. When my gaze met Tam's and caught him smiling, too, I knew exactly what I'd say when I called Kellen.

———

Once again, I found myself facing my supervisor across the desk in his office. I'd requested a face-to-face meeting as soon as he'd picked up the phone and flown straight here, but now that I sat in front of him, figuring out what to say was another matter altogether. I didn't doubt he'd read the report by now, but that had been the professional version of the events of the past few days. Kellen hadn't witnessed the parts Tam had left out.

Kellen studied my face. "Perry. I'm glad to see you survived losing your Wi-Fi connection for a full day."

And just like that, we were back to normal. "Ha ha. I think the tower might need a backup generator in case the power goes out at a time of crisis again. Is there someone in the department I can pester for that one?"

"I'll pass the message on," Kellen said. "Am I to conclude that you hit it off with your new teammates?"

"It was a bit of a rocky start," I admitted. "Took a while to get on the same page, and there were issues with certain team members' abilities..."

"That was always a risk for everyone involved," Kellen said. "I didn't think I'd have any luck placing you with a *normal* team, but Tam's lot are good people, despite being a little different."

"You've personally worked with all of them before?" I guessed. "Tam said… you told him about the curse. And my past."

"I hope you'll forgive me for that," he said. "I asked him to keep it quiet, but I wanted the team leader to be aware in case…"

"In case it turned out to be an issue later on?" I guessed. "It almost did, but after the possessed tree, the others came to the decision that a little curse was nothing in comparison."

"I thought not," he said. "I still hold out hope of finding a solution to your problem, but I hoped you'd feel more settled if you had people around you who've faced similar challenges. It took a while to find the right team, and like I said, the others have had their own issues, ones I won't get into."

"Hmm." My head still buzzed with questions, particularly concerning Tam's own abilities, but I'd prefer to gain Tam's trust myself rather than go behind his back. "I heard they lost a member last year. My predecessor. Is that why there was a vacancy?"

"Ah." He grimaced. "Yes. The poor girl's death was a tragic accident, but it hit Tam particularly hard, as team leader."

I supposed it must have. I scraped at the back of my mind for a way to ask what had happened to her without coming across as insensitive. It helped that the rest of the team wasn't present, and Kellen wouldn't judge me, no matter what I said.

"I wish I'd known before I asked," I mumbled. "Though I understand why you didn't tell me."

"I knew there was a mind-reader on the team who'd

realise I'd betrayed their trust if I told you their secrets," he said. "It wasn't an easy call to make."

"Oh." I hadn't even thought that might be the reason. "You knew about his habit of sticking his psychic abilities where they don't belong?"

"No, but I had an inkling you might push his buttons, given your history with vampires."

Guilty. "So, you threw me to the sharks without warning."

"No, I decided to let you judge him for yourself."

"And I screwed up spectacularly."

"Nobody got staked to death, did they?"

"There were a few close calls." I shook my head. "All right, I get it. He's sworn to keep out of my thoughts on Tam's orders, so it's safe to tell me all his secrets."

"Nice try." He smiled briefly and then his expression turned serious. "I can tell you what happened to your predecessor ... to Clarice. If, that is, you don't mention it to the others unless they bring it up first."

"I won't," I said. "But I'm guessing it'll explain why they all reacted like I'd summoned that tree demon when I first walked into the tower and tried to use a conjuring spell to fetch my suitcase."

"Ah." He grimaced. "I didn't realise that might be an issue."

"I would've used the spell outside if the heavens hadn't opened on my head," I said. "They were fine with me using magic to help solve the murder, though. What's the deal?"

"Clarice..." He paused. "She was a witch, like you, who specialised in hunting down monsters. She was very good at it too. I didn't work with her directly, but by all accounts, she was both personable and good at her job."

Ouch. I wouldn't lie, his words stirred a pang of jealousy that I sternly squashed down.

"But?" I prompted. "What happened to her?"

"It was a routine mission," he began. "The team went to stay in a village farther to the north, where they were hunting a creature that could possess people."

Oh, boy. I could guess where this might be going. "A demonic spirit, right?"

"Exactly," he said. "When they isolated its host, the creature escaped. Unbeknownst to the others, it latched on to Clarice."

My mouth went dry. "So … so it possessed and killed her?"

"No, it possessed her and caused her to turn against the rest of the team," he said. "She attacked them. They barely got out of their house before it went up in flames, and she was left trapped inside."

"Oh, no."

"Tam was lucky he didn't suffocate while he was trying to get her out," he said. "It was too late, though. She used her last bit of strength to cast a banishment spell to send the creature back to the afterworld before she died."

The incident must have been more traumatic for the rest of the team than I'd realised. It certainly explained why they'd reacted the way they had to suddenly obtaining a new member.

"That's awful," I whispered.

"That's why it took the others a while to warm to the idea of taking on someone else," he said. "In the end, I only got Tam to agree, and he said that the others would find it easier to actually meet you before making a commitment."

"Yeah." I blinked hard. "If that's what I have to live up to, I'll try not to be too much of a disappointment."

He tilted his head. "That makes it sound like you plan to stay."

"I thought that was a given." I met my supervisor's gaze. "What was the alternative? Move back to another city and terrorise the local vampires?"

"If you wanted to," he said. "Like I said, I wanted to give you a chance to experience being part of a team, but the choice is ultimately yours alone."

"I know." I shifted in my seat. "I think I want to give it a shot."

His craggy face looked surprised and pleased. "You're really sure? Even about being on the same team as a vampire?"

"We're never going to be BFFs, I can say that much," I said. "The others, though … we're getting on fine."

After sending off our report the previous evening, we'd spent the night playing a riotous game of Cards Against Humanity and watching terrible horror movies. I'd had worse evenings.

"Good." He smiled. "Then you should head back and let them know, shouldn't you?"

"I think they already do." I rose to my feet.

Time to return to the castle, where my team would be waiting to prepare for our next mission.

ABOUT THE AUTHOR

Elle Adams lives in the middle of England, where she spends most of her time reading an ever-growing mountain of books, planning her next adventure, or writing. Elle's books are humorous mysteries with a paranormal twist, packed with magical mayhem.

She also writes urban and contemporary fantasy novels as Emma L. Adams.

Visit http://www.elleadamsauthor.com/ to find out more about Elle's books.

www.ingramcontent.com/pod-product-compliance
Lightning Source LLC
Chambersburg PA
CBHW020814190726
48285CB00006B/2277